After graduating from the University of Oklahoma (oh – so long ago), David bolted to Los Angeles to find something – anything – different from the red-dirt predictability of his native land. In California, he eventually found his niche – writing advertising, TV comedies, and dozens upon dozens of live corporate stage productions.

Decades later, David returned to his Oklahoma roots to be warmly greeted by family and long-lost friends, plus the cold reality of a pandemic...which gave him more than enough time to write.

Hence, came up his first novel – *Medicine Park*.

Looking back over a long life, I dedicate this novel to everyone I've ever known.

That said, I wish I'd gotten around more.

David Curry

MEDICINE PARK

A Metaphysical Murder Mystery

AUSTIN MACAULEY PUBLISHERS™

LONDON • CAMBRIDGE • NEW YORK • SHARJAH

Ordering Information
Quantity sales: Special discounts are available on quantity purchases by corporations, associations, and others. For details, contact the publisher at the address below.

Publisher's Cataloging-in-Publication data
Curry, David
Medicine Park

ISBN 9781685627133 (Paperback)
ISBN 9781685627140 (Hardback)
ISBN 9781685627157 (ePub e-book)

Library of Congress Control Number: 2023913117

www.austinmacauley.com/us

First Published 2024
Austin Macauley Publishers LLC
40 Wall Street, 33rd Floor, Suite 3302
New York, NY 10005
USA

mail-usa@austinmacauley.com
+1 (646) 5125767

Heartfelt thanks to my wife and partner, Alice, for her encouragement and comradery during the long hours I spent writing *Medicine Park*. It was comforting to know I was not alone.

Table of Contents

Storm Clouds

"We may have all come on different ships, but we're in the same boat now."

Martin Luther King
August 28, 1963

They told me to give you my name, right up front…along with what they call *pertinent biographical information.*

So, Herman Lace, 48. And in the spirit of full disclosure, rapidly aging. I suppose you'd consider me average build and…Caucasian. Is that the correct term nowadays? Oh, and I'm losing a significant amount of hair. Which people tend to notice.

Anyway, I've taught History at Medicine Park High for over 25 years; one of the many reasons I drink.

You would, too, if you had to corral a bunch of goddam TV addicts. Darwin had it backward. Before long, they'll come to class dragging their knuckles on the ground.

I'll never understand why kids get hooked on those TV westerns. Gunsmoke, Wagon Train, Cheyenne. Gives 'em a mighty cock-eyed view of frontier life. Dumb cowboys and Indians shoot-'em-up stuff.

To get a sense of what *real* Indians were like back then, look no farther than our own Quanah Parker here in Comanche County. His mother was a white girl from east Texas kidnapped by a band of marauders. She ended up marrying the chieftain who snatched her. Go figure that one.

They raised their oldest boy, Quanah, to lead the fight against the white settlers and army troops who poached their land and slaughtered their buffalo.

I tell my students, over and over: The story of civilization is about adaptation and transcendence.

Quanah Parker knew the score.

He wound up becoming chief of all Plains Indian tribes. Then, when faced with the inevitable, he brokered peace with the white man. He quickly switched from warrior, to rancher and statesman. Hell, when he wasn't traveling to

Washington, he was on reservation land near the Wichita mountains, hunting wolves with the likes of Teddy Roosevelt!

Adaptation and transcendence. Chief Parker knew when to pivot and roll with the tide. You know, I see our *entire country* struggling with that right now. Things are like a speedboat lurching forward and moving faster. I know, because I read it every Sunday in the *New York Times*.

Folks here in Medicine Park don't see the big picture. They've lived here all their lives, but they have *no idea* what goes on beneath the surface.

I know that sounds harsh. It's only a small Okie resort town, so what do you expect, right? But you'd think they'd see the pattern in all the wild events that have happened these past weeks, starting when the fish in Founder's Lake disappeared. A real death-knell for tourism, I'd say. Followed by a grisly murder, with reporters from all over the country swooping in. The kind of tourists we don't need.

That, plus one of our most respected citizens, Chief Quanah Parker's great-grandson, Sampson Whitefeather is still nowhere to be found.

They're all symptoms of a larger national malaise, if you ask *me*. I mean, some crazy bastard in Dallas just shot our President three times – pow – right through the noggin. From a schoolbook depository window, it turns out. I'm still scratching my head over that one.

It feels like the world is on the verge of insanity. And in my humble opinion, *another* good reason to drink.

Herman T. Lace
Medicine Park, Oklahoma
November 25, 1963

"The real 1960s began on the afternoon of November 22, 1963. Kennedy's murder opened some malign trap door in American culture, and wild bats flapped out."

Author Lance Morrow
Time Magazine

Sampson Parker Whitefeather stood back from his yellow 1940s Boeing-Stearman 75 biplane, admiring the freshly painted red letters across its fuselage:

"Sky Chief."

It was a far cry from the F9F fighter jet he commandeered during dozens of sorties over North Korean airspace in the early '50s. But as crop dusters go, the old 75 was up to the task, modified with a bowl-shaped aluminum hopper – a stout container for liquid pesticide – welded below the cockpit. The plane's powerful Pratt & Whitney R-985 engine and constant-speed propeller upped the maximum take-off weight by nearly 1,700 pounds – a necessity for a faded duster with 192 gallons of DDT fuel-oil solution strapped to its underbelly.

This bright and cloudless May morning was, as usual, dedicated to Sampson's meticulous preflight fuel and instrument checks and rechecks. One look at this intense 41-year-old Native American with a commanding, weathered face, and lean six-foot frame confirmed why everyone in Comanche County called him Sky Chief. His long, shoulder-length dark hair was usually tied into a ponytail, and his faded gray Stetson hat was his crowning signature.

Most locals considered Sampson Whitefeather a war hero. Perhaps his greatest feat was his emergency landing near the bridge over North Korea's Yalu River, to pull Navy pilot and childhood buddy, Captain Ben Thomas, from the smoldering wreckage of his gunned-down F-51 Mustang.

It was an act of extraordinary valor – one handsomely repaid six years after the war, when Thomas was elected Mayor of Medicine Park. Skirting exclusionary local property laws, he bequeathed Lieutenant Whitefeather 48 acres of his founding family's prime real estate on the east side of Lake Lawtonka, three miles north of town.

Most Comanches were forced to live on federal land – euphemistically called 'reservations.' Whitefeather, however, considered his gifted acreage to be community property, and he made parcels available to tribespeople for collective gardening, horse stabling, and spiritual gatherings.

These all-night spiritual ceremonies were a vital feature of the Native American Church – indigenous, peyote-induced rituals mixed with traditional Christian teachings. But as Sampson was fond of saying, "The white man goes into his church and talks about Jesus. The Indian goes into his tipi and talks *to* Jesus."

The Whitefeather compound is a mile east of Lake Lawtonka, across north-south highway 58. The family's white, two-story clapboard house is a replica of Chief Quanah Parker's 'Star Home' – a popular tourist attraction in the neighboring town of Cache.

This spring morning, as Sampson completes maintenance checks on his Boeing 75, he notices his wife Nina in the distance, standing on their front porch. Nina Parker Whitefeather usually adhered to her tribal Comanche roots, preferring knee-length buckskin dresses, adorned with colorful beadwork. She braided her long jet-black hair into two thick strands, secured with ribbons.

Uh oh, Sampson thinks as he sees their oldest son, 17-year-old Blaze, join his wife on the porch. Blaze had been nothing but trouble – *even before he was born*. Early in Nina's pregnancy, she was bitten by a timber rattlesnake, an incident Sampson viewed as an evil omen after a tribal shaman summoned 'coyote spirits' while applying chewed plantain weed to her ankle wound.

"Bad medicine," Sampson later told her obstetrician at the county community health center. And he believed Nina's months-long bouts of restless nights and feverish dreams proved him right.

Now, watching his wife and son heading in his direction, Sampson anxiously rubs the side of his biplane like an airborne talisman, wondering if there was enough time for him to leap into the cockpit and get his baby off the ground before they could reach him.

He senses a family confrontation as they continue walking toward him, past the horse corral and the communal gardens, with its bounty of corn, pumpkin, squash, and spineless cactus – crowned by pink and yellowish peyote flowers.

He absently pulls on the sides of his dungarees as wife and son pass the unpainted barn, the small aircraft maintenance shed and several canvass-covered tipis that were used for community rituals.

As they draw closer, Sampson's eyes now fix on Blaze. He's dressed in cuffed Levi jeans, a short-sleeved sport shirt and penny loafers without socks – which Sampson suspects is the current uniform of teenage white boys. Although Blaze started his educational regimen at the nearby Fort Sill Indian Boarding School, his recent transfer to the public Medicine Park High is causing new frictions.

Sampson supported Nina's constant efforts to get Blaze to wear dress pants and socks and, importantly, keep his shirttails tucked in. He disapproved of his son's unruly dark brown hair, which had grown much too long for conforming Anglo sensibilities.

Sky Chief knows all-too-well the subject of this inevitable family powwow: Last night, his wife told him she caught Blaze in their barn, smoking tobacco and chewing peyote buttons with two of his school friends. This is troubling for so many reasons! Peyote is for adult spiritual use, not teenage recreation. How could Sampson alter his son's impulsive behavior? Should he call for a special tribal service, conducted by their elder, Big Sandman – with intensive prayer and chanting to chase away Blaze's contrary spirits? Or should he mimic white Christian culture and take a leather strap to the boy?

"What do you say?" Nina challenges Sampson, a heartbeat after they arrive.

Sampson wisely takes a deep breath before speaking. "Son, what will it take to change your contrary path?"

Blaze blinks rapidly, his eyes darting back and forth between his mother and father. "Well, this morning I was thinking…maybe if I had my own drums. Learning to play might focus my mind."

This pleases Sampson: Pounding ceremonial drums might be a rightful channeling of Blaze's manic spirits, a purposeful activity to keep him from flapping into trouble like a wild bat.

"He seems possessed by this idea of drums," Nina adds.

Sampson leans in. "Son, by drums you mean like our sacramental iron tubs with beaver skin covering?"

Blaze hesitates. "Uh, not exactly. I was thinking more like rack 'n' floor toms, with bass and snare. You know, for a cool Beach Boys' sound."

Sampson's face falls and his mind quickly drifts. For the first time in nearly 100 years, since the dark day his great grandfather made peace with his white subjugators, Sky Chief senses the inevitable death of their tribal ways.

"I Fall to Pieces."

Patsy Cline
Kansas City, Kansas
March 5, 1963

Herman Lace again – with a word to the wise: Don't let your kids get hooked on those goddamn transistor radios! I have nothing against today's music, you understand. But students are bringing those little plastic gadgets to school, and it's only a matter of time before they start sneaking 'em into the classroom. That's where I put my foot down.

My daughter, Brenda, wants me to buy her one. I hate the idea of it. But since me and my wife are in the middle of a divorce, I'll let *her* play the bad cop!

So. Now that we're on the subject, my soon-to-be ex, Carol, went back to Illinois to live with her sister, whose husband just died of lung cancer. My daughter's spending the summer with them. Good for her, I suppose. She's latched onto the dead man's piano and seems to be developing a keen interest in music.

Brenda tells me she's learned several new songs by people I've never heard of *except*, on a recent phone call, she played me a tune by Patsy Cline, who I happen to like. It's unfortunate – Patsy's death in that plane crash. Last March, I think it was. I read where it was one of those small Piper Cubs, returning from a concert. All I can say is it puts a nasty spin on her big hit, *I Fall to Pieces.*

Sad to say, lots of folks I know seem to be falling apart including my estranged, Carol, who's having her share of mental problems. Which, I'm told, I can't discuss. But it makes me wonder whether she has a leg to stand on, in terms of getting custody of Brenda. My lawyer tells me there's a fighting chance she'll be back with me for her senior year. I sure hope so because I'm saving for a piano.

It was no secret: Brenda Lace hated her given name and preferred being called 'Bren.' And during the three months she and her mother lived with her aunt Doris in Benton, Illinois, the townsfolk gladly parroted 'Bren' back to her. The new handle was one of the many ways this Illinois summer gave Bren a chance to toss her tiny-town Okie baggage, including her quirky and judgmental father back home.

Unfortunately, her Benton reinvention is coming to an end. Her mom, Carol, is fighting anxiety and depression with medication and counseling. Her distress, however, is escalating: After her second arrest for shoplifting, the Comanche County court ordered Bren back into Herman Lace's custody until her 18th birthday…a seems-like-forever nine months away.

This emotional crossfire wounds Bren and exacerbates her rebellious nature. Her too-cool style and attitude favored thrift store print dresses, cowboy boots, white plastic sunglasses, and lace gloves. Her signature accessory: a sequin-covered shoulder bag containing loose bills, a small notebook, guitar picks, and a tobacco pouch with American Spirit rolling papers. She drew curious double takes wherever she went. Which was the idea.

With a population of around 7,000 – mostly blue collar, mostly white – Benton Illinois is a five-hour drive southeast of Chicago. It's as Midwestern friendly and earnest as you can find: a sulfur-coal and railroad town with a charming Main Street roundabout.

Despite significant differences between Bren's Medicine Park origins and her recently-adopted Benton, they are both delicate ecosystems that revel in ah-shucks gossip. And tonight, the buzz centers on a last-minute get-together at Louise Harrison's house, around the corner from the high school. Louise is excited that her two younger brothers are visiting from England, and she wants her neighbors to meet them.

This includes Bren, who thinks a British invasion sounds exciting.

By 9:00 PM, the Harrison's narrow two-story brick home is packed. Bren begins the evening in a jovial, social mood but soon lets the thought of her impending bus ride back to Okie-land bring her down. She wanders away from the hubbub, finds two empty wrought iron chairs in the far corner of the backyard, and begins rolling a cigarette from her tobacco pouch.

Now what? she thinks, over and over. *Now what? Now what?* She's jolted from her reverie by a distinctive voice.

"Looks good!"

Bren lifts her eyes to see a thin young man with surprisingly long dark hair, resembling a mop, with bangs down to his eyebrows. He wears a paisley sport shirt, tight black jeans, and ankle-length leather boots.

He points to her tobacco pouch. "Roll me one of those ciggies?"

"Sure." Bren indicates the empty chair beside her. "Have a seat. I'm Bren."

"George here. You look a bit young to be smoking," he says, sliding the chair closer to her. He notes that she looks more eccentric than the other local birds, and her large brown eyes immediately attract him.

Bren shrugs. "Do I?"

"How old are you, anyway?"

Bren figures George to be around 20, thinks about fudging her own age a bit, then decides it's best to go with the truth, "17."

George laughs. "She was just 17! My bandmates wrote a song about that."

"You write songs?" Bren says, pleasantly surprised. "Me too. On the piano and guitar. I should say *I'm trying to*. They probably suck."

"Well, the first ones usually *are* shat. You just gotta keep at it."

Bren hands George a freshly rolled cigarette and gives him an appraising look. He's cute! "I, uh, love your hair. Never seen that style before. Whaddaya call it?"

"Arthur." He gives her a playful wink.

Bren laughs, thankful for his attention. "Louise tells me you're from England."

"She's a sharp one, she is. Indeed, here with my brother Peter on holiday. First time in America. Bloody good folks I'd say. You from around here?"

"Nope. A place in Oklahoma called Medicine Park. Funny name, huh?"

"Hey, you're talking to a bloke from *Liverpool*."

"Good point."

George checks her out, lighting his cigarette and taking a deep drag. "You seem a bit distracted. What's up?"

"I'm okay. It's just I gotta go back home tomorrow. So, I'm kinda bummed. People are way too closed-minded there."

"That so?"

"I mean, I don't think they really see me."

"Hmm." George considers this as he exhales a stream of smoke. "You know I think the important thing is for *you* to see who you really are. Find *that*, then tune into it and let it guide you. You'll be okay."

Bren nods, thoughtfully. "Thanks, George. I'll remember that." She blows a smoke ring. "You know, I'd love to hear your band sometime."

"Oh, you will." He grins. "We've got the #1 record in England, and we're coming for you buggers in America."

With that, George excuses himself and walks into the house. He returns, moments later, to present Bren with a 45-rpm pressing of the Beatles' new hit – *She Loves You!*

It's a song that will launch the next chapter of her life.

"We choose to go to the Moon in this decade and do the other things, not because they are easy, but because they are hard."

President John F. Kennedy
September 12, 1962

Me again. You know, every year I teach my kids about the 19th-century doctrine of Manifest Destiny...our mission to shove Christianity and capitalism down people's throats, from sea to shining sea.

I call it our *delusional suicide pact*, the compulsion to spread our perceived moral virtue like a poisonous Johnny Appleseed.

We honestly believe God wants us to win. And as insane as that sounds, I'm afraid it's calcified in our bones. We've built our national identity on being bigger, stronger, better; on being number one.

Now, I don't confront my students in such stark terms. I soften it quite a bit. I *do* want to keep my job.

What I'd *like* to tell them in the 100 years since the 'destiny' idea was coined, we've continuously been at war for other people's land – first the Mexicans and Spanish, then the Indians. And lately we've turned our attention to the American Negro, trying to keep 'em in their place, if not drive 'em back to where they came from.

Exhibit A: Last week in Birmingham, the Klan killed four Negro girls in a church bombing. Colored folks in Alabama *still* can't use public restrooms, eat in diners or attend the university. And I hasten to add: things aren't any better around *these parts.*

Here's my point: Instead of fighting hatred and racism in our own backyard, we've decided to fight communism instead. *All over the world.* And if that's not bad enough, our president keeps telling us we need to win the space race.

I'm scratching my head over that one. Since when did our quest for meaning translate to conquering everything that's *out there?*

It's like Jack Kerouac said in his novel *On the Road:* 'After all my travels, I have nothing to offer anybody, except my own confusion.'

He gave us a warning, but we're not listening. After nearly two hundred years of war and expansionism, we're still hooked on new conquests and the lure of the open highway. But we can't find the truth if we're lost in our own backyard.

Herman T. Lace
September 27, 1963

Jonny Sparks is upset for a shit-load of reasons.

The biggest: He's flat on his back on the 5th floor of the St. Louis University Hospital, recovering from a tonsillectomy. It hurts like hell to swallow! But there's *another* fact to swallow: the surgery threatens his impending road trip with his friend Steve, a couple weeks before the start of their senior year.

If that isn't the shits, his grandparents just flew in from Oklahoma, and they're camped out, along with his mom and dad, in his hospital room. It's awful!

"Jonny," his mother says, refereeing the contest for his affection, "play nice."

"I'm sorry, Grandma," he whispers to the tiny lady hovering beside his bed like a nervous hummingbird. He wants to tell her that she has too much powder on her face. "I wasn't ignoring you; it just hurts to talk."

"I hope it doesn't ruin that beautiful voice of yours!" his Grandma Ruby replies, squeezing his hand. "I want you to get well, so you can come and visit soon. Seems like forever since you've been to Medicine Park."

Behind her, Grandpa Lester gazes absently out the window at what he considers a crazed, mind-boggling metropolis. He's still wearing his worn Fedora hat. "Well, we're together *now*," Jonny's mother says, taking charge. She turns to her husband, Richard, standing by the door. "Hon, why don't you drive mom and dad home and get 'em settled in? And take Route 40, it's faster."

"What about *you*?" Richard says, sounding victimized.

"You can come back for me in an hour or so. I want to get Jonny a milkshake from the cafeteria. Doesn't that sound good, dear?" she says, squeezing Jonny's hand.

Richard Sparks was fighting a foul mood; he had indigestion earlier at work, and he felt light-headed several times throughout the day. But he's determined to be a good soldier, at least for a few hours more. Past that, all bets are off.

After Jonny's dad and grandparents clear the room, his mother, Janet, gets down to business.

"You're *not* going *anywhere* with Steve Fletcher," she says, adamantly. "Much less on a cross-county trip."

"Why?" Jonny replies in a pained, raspy voice.

"*Oh, let me count the ways*! Surely you don't think I'm letting you drive to California with that numbskull…who, I might add, has a DUI."

"He wasn't drunk."

"And he was expelled for fighting last semester. I know what goes on at school."

"He didn't throw the first punch."

"He has no self-control, no common sense. The answer is no."

Janet Sparks is overly protective of Jonny, because she believes she failed to protect *herself* for so many years. After working her way through the University of Oklahoma School of Journalism and landing an internship at the St. Louis Post-Dispatch, Janet knowingly thwarted her career, seeking the approval of leering, piggish male co-workers, and patronizing editorial managers. She wondered, how many years would she allow her reporting to be limited to weddings and bar mitzvahs and home & garden events?

She constantly second-guessed her decision to chuck it all and marry Richard, the Post's retail advertising manager, whose office was on the floor below hers. Settling for a man on a lower floor was just too symbolic, she constantly reminds herself, even years after Jonny was born and she'd suffered two subsequent miscarriages.

And now that she's decided to return to the workforce, she's hosting the very folks who consistently failed to support her over the years – starting the day she told them she wanted to go away to college.

She laughs at the notion, but decides to file it away. For now, once again. How difficult would it be to keep her mouth shut for another week?

Where the hell is Richard? Janet thinks to herself after returning to Jonny's room, chocolate milkshake in hand.

It was nearly 7:30 and it would soon be dark.

She turns on the TV across from Jonny's bed and is immediately grabbed by a 'just breaking' news report from local CBS affiliate, KMOV: A head-on crash on Route 40 has claimed the lives of five people. Three were passengers inside a blue '61 Ford Galaxy, whose driver inexplicably swerved into oncoming traffic and front-ended a white Chevy sedan. "Oh my God," Janet screams, startling Jonny. "That's our car!" Two ambulances were on the scene, with paramedics loading covered bodies into the rear of the vehicles.

Janet would soon learn from the autopsy report that her husband, Richard, had a massive heart attack and lost consciousness behind the wheel. Four innocent people also died. Two were her mom and dad. If it weren't for her son, Jonny, she would have gladly joined them.

"I am not going to lose Vietnam. I am not going to be the president who saw Southeast Asia go the way China went."

President Lyndon Johnson
To Ambassador Henry Cabot Lodge
November 24, 1963

Back again...and I'm compelled to say, I feel storm clouds coming. I mean, for *all of us*. I don't share this with my students; they have enough problems and anxieties at their age. But I think you can handle it.

Earlier, I expressed skepticism about our national obsession with *Manifest Destiny*, our perceived greatness, and our willingness to fight for it. But frankly, my concern extends beyond that misguided nonsense.

My sense of ill winds blowing is partly based on what my oldest, Paul, tells me. He's my 'canary in the coal mine' so to speak – an army corporal, stationed just a few miles south at Fort Sill in Lawton. *It's a field artillery base.* And now, Paul has constant headaches from hearing those loud guns going off, morning and night. I'm talking about cannons and howitzers and rocket launchers. Tons and tons of new hardware coming in.

And why is that? Just a theory but last Sunday, I read in the *New York Times* where Washington politicians are doubling down on North Vietnam. They call it 'escalation' which could explain the recent quantity of my drinking.

I guess the Pentagon thinks hundreds of military advisors aren't enough. We can't let those Chinese communists run amok, can't let those dominoes fall. I swear, the moment LBJ was sworn in, Ho Chi Minh got a huge target on his back.

I'm starting to worry about *our* boys in uniform. It feels like we're heading for a new season of insanity. My daughter, Brenda (who now prefers to be called Bren, by the way) tells me I'm jumping to conclusions. *Maybe.* But I'm a student of American history. And I've seen this story play out too many times.

Sampson Whitefeather is in full warrior mode. After filling the spray tank of his crop duster at a refueling site near the Red River, he's back to cruising altitude for a final top spraying sprint before continuing north toward his Comanche County home.

While former Lieutenant Whitefeather and his great grandfather, Chief Quanah Parker, shared a fierce, combative spirit in their youth, they were also late-life architects of white appeasement.

In truth, Sampson Whitefeather led two distinct lives: One is on the ground in Medicine Park, where he's a token of decorum and status-quo citizenship, keeping his tribe integrated into the white Christian community. Up in the air, however, Sampson lets Quanah's 'warrior blood' flow through his veins – often smearing his face with war paint and pretending to dump hundreds of gallons of chemical fury on those who slaughtered and oppressed his people.

Sampson clearly sees the whimsy in these pesticide fantasies. He also has the good sense to keep them to himself.

On this particularly muggy and blustery June afternoon, Sampson the 'Sky Chief' senses a threatening storm front moving in. He surveys the dark, greenish clouds rapidly moving toward him, several miles from the east. Leaves and branches churn along the ground below.

What seems like a heartbeat later, Sampson's vintage bi-plane is buffeted by severe gusts of wind, followed by a shower of baseball-sized hailstones pounding its wings.

Bam! Whack! A large chunk of ice crashes into the propeller – halting its spin and sending shards of metal into the air.

As Sampson anxiously searches the ground for a spot to land, he feels the ominous, otherworldly force of a tornado funnel approaching his plane.

Can I get down? he wonders, trying to remain calm, trying to stay in hyper-focused combat mode. Could he wrestle his wounded craft to the ground without it busting into pieces?

Those were Sampson Whitefeather's last thoughts on that calamitous afternoon.

His mind suddenly freezes when a flying chunk of ice crashes into his right temple, sending his gray Stetson skyward.

The lights go out as churning storm clouds engulf his plane.

Thunderbolts

"The times, they are a-changin'."

Bob Dylan
Greenwich Village, NY
December 1963

John William Elmer Thomas, an Indiana-born lawyer and real estate developer, founded Medicine Park in 1908. He named it for the wide creek that snaked through the center of town. Nestled in the foothills of the Wichita Mountains, Thomas envisioned a popular resort to capitalize on the medicinal qualities of the creek – benefits long touted by the indigenous Kiowa, Apache, and Comanche nations.

What started as a simple resort quickly became a vacation getaway for both the famous and the infamous – from Teddy Roosevelt and Will Rogers to Al Capone, Pretty Boy Floyd, and Bonnie & Clyde.

After its founder, JWE Thomas, was elected to the U.S. senate in 1926, he sold the park to Stringer & Partners; Dallas-based oil wildcatters who banked on the strategy of 'boom or bust.' This go-for-broke mentality foreshadowed the fate of Medicine Park.

At its peak in 1941, over 200,000 visitors flocked to the town each year to enjoy its unique cobblestone streets and walls, nearby lakes, spas, and diverse mountain wildlife. But due to lack of vision, investment, and the advent of World War II, the community began to decline. By 1963, only 683 people remained.

Recent events only added to the residents' collective anxiety – including a drop-off in tourist revenue. And the town *still* hasn't recovered from the mid-summer tornado that ripped through the post office and chewed up portions of the Oklahoma Press Association clubhouse and historic Medicine Park Hotel.

But now, like the U.S. Calvary riding to the rescue, the grandson of Medicine Park's founder is stepping up.

Ben Thomas, Mayor of Medicine Park, is conducting a rare press event in the lobby of Lawton's Comanche County Courthouse. It's the county seat, 14 miles south of his hometown. He thoughtfully surveys the 30-plus onlookers awaiting his remarks.

This *must* go over big – the local KSWO television crew is there! And to the right of Ben's podium, a tall sculptural object – covered in silk fabric – provides even greater anticipation.

"Welcome, everyone! Thanks for coming. I want to say, right up top, I recognize times have been tough around these parts especially for my constituents up the road in Medicine Park. But I'm here to announce: *Times are changing!*"

Ben measures his audience, then hunches his six-foot-four frame over the podium for emphasis. "Medicine Park is dangling from a cliff! We don't have enough students to keep our school going. We don't have the circulation to keep our newspaper running. We don't have the money to keep our town operating." He pauses, dramatically. "*Until now.*"

Wondering if his remarks are landing, he adjusts his pale green tie, which blends with his bright green sport coat. Ben loves the Master's Golf Tournament, and it shows. His green-tinted snakeskin boots are simply the kicker.

He pushes forward with as much gusto as he can summon. "I've joined an investor group. Think of us as *silent partners* and our first order of business is expanding Medicine Park. We're buying a large tract of land east of town – out toward Elgin. Our goal is to quickly break ground on a new shopping center and housing development. We also plan to be up and running with a new version of Medicine High by the '66 school year. Until then, we're merging with Elgin's school, beginning this January."

Ben pushes his rusty blond hair back over his ears and waits for his words to sink in. "So for the immediate future, the Fighting Falcons will become the Mighty Owls! And they'll continue to be coached by our own head man, Carter Singleton."

Mayor Thomas glances around, looking for the coach.

"Ready, willing, and more-than-able!" Carter whoops loudly from the back of the room, acknowledging those turning to check out his red and tan letter jacket and matching ball cap.

The mayor grins. "Carter, I know you're anxious to win us another Division 3 football championship. And now you'll have a new pool of students to recruit from. So, I don't think it's too early to say go Owls, win state!"

Ben Thomas can feel it: the room is his!

"Now," he continues, "a couple more things. First, the publisher of the Medicine Park newspaper, Vic Chandler, is retiring and closing the Gazette after 20 spectacular years. And, going forward, we plan to consolidate our news with the Elgin Chronicle."

Ben pauses to visualize his grandfather and muster needed emotion. "This year marks the 55th anniversary of Medicine Park's founding in 1908. And to commemorate the occasion, we're printing a special edition of the Gazette, right before Christmas. It'll be its final publication, and a fitting way to close it out."

He takes a deep breath before heading to the finish line. "The number 55 has always been special to me. Aside from my golf handicap" – he grins – *"just kidding.* It was the number on the side of my fighter jet during the Korean War. Many of you know, I was shot down and pulled from my burning plane by fellow Navy pilot and childhood friend, Sampson Whitefeather. Now he's gone. After three gut-wrenching months, searching for clues to his disappearance, we're no closer today than we were the afternoon his plane was swept from the sky. But we continue to pray and hope for the best. He was loved and respected by all."

The mayor turns to indicate the tall covered object to his right. "To help us honor his memory, I've asked his lovely wife, Nina, to join me to present a special work of art, an original sculpture, crafted by fellow Comanche tribe members Dan and Tala Birdsong."

Ben grabs the gray silk cover and gingerly pulls it away – revealing an eight-foot wooden bow, decorated with an array of white whooping-crane feathers. The piece is both deeply touching and profoundly strange.

Nina joins the mayor at the podium, holding a small black booklet. She waits for the ambient noise in the room to die down before speaking. "Thank you for your good wishes today. My husband kept a diary. He was faithful to it. And I will now share his last words, written the night before his final flight."

She clears her throat, then begins reading. "Most white people I know have tense faces. They are always seeking something. But what? They seem uneasy and restless. I have no idea what they want. *I think they are mad!*"

Nina looks out into the audience, as confused as anyone about Sampson's departing sentiments. She shrugs. "That's where he stopped."

Betty Allen has served as Medicine Park's high school principal for over five years. She's been the choir director at Park Baptist Church for seven. But on this warm Sunday afternoon in September, she's fulfilling her *life-long* role as Good Samaritan.

Pretty Betty, tinfoil-covered casserole dish in hand, walks the two short blocks from her home on East Longhorn Avenue to Merry Circle Drive – arriving at the modest two-bedroom, cobblestone-walled home of the late Lester and Ruby Sparks.

Ascending the steep front steps, Betty – a bit out of breath – reaches the warped front door with peeling white paint. She clutches the casserole tightly as she knocks. She waits a few moments, then knocks again. She waits. Patience is one of Betty's defining virtues. Finally, the door slowly opens to reveal Janet Sparks, wrapped in a navy-blue terrycloth bathrobe. Her short, chestnut-colored hair is arranged in what could be called 'early afternoon bed-head.'

"Yes?" Janet says, scrutinizing Betty, who's still wearing her dressy church clothes. Janet's gaze fixes on Betty's pink pillbox hat.

"It's me, hon. Betty! We talked yesterday at the cemetery."

"Cemetery?"

"Highland. In Lawton. At your mom and dad's funeral."

It finally sinks in. "Oh. I'm sorry." Janet flashes a weak, embarrassed smile. "It was such a crazy day."

"Sure it was! And I loved meeting your lovely son, Jonny." Janet self-consciously tightens up her robe as Betty holds out the glass dish. "I thought you'd like some tuna casserole. It's one of my specialties, if I do say so myself!"

"…Thank you. Thank you, Betty," Janet replies, trying to compose herself as she hesitantly opens the door. "Please come in."

"Oh, I don't want to be a bother."

"No bother. Come in. I could use some company."

Betty gingerly steps into the tacky, sparsely furnished front room. Several large cardboard boxes and tape rolls are strewn about, and it appears Janet is packing up some of her parent's possessions. Janet takes the casserole bowl from Betty and gestures for her to sit down on the worn, cloth-covered sofa.

Betty's face lights up as she notices the only picture left hanging on the wall, directly across from her. "*Oh, I love that*, Jesus praying in the Garden of Gethsemane."

Janet glances at the faded print image inside a stained wooden frame, hung much too high for her taste. "Yes, the garden. Mom loved that. I keep thinking it's a metaphor for something."

Betty gives her a bewildered look. "Metaphor? I don't think so hon. Jesus is simply inviting us to share in God's grace."

Janet stares at Betty for an uncomfortably long time before switching gears. "Weren't you a couple of grades behind me in school? I think I remember you, but it's all a bit of a blur."

"Well, I sure remember *you*! I always thought you'd make a splash, you know, after graduation. You didn't come back very often. I wish you had."

Janet moves to the adjacent dining nook and sets the casserole on the table. "Probably not as much as I should've."

Betty smiles, winks. "Well, I hope you're not holding a grudge."

"I think it had more to do with my relationship with mom and dad than, you know, how I feel about Medicine Park."

"Well, I hope you'll stay for a while this time. We could use your get-up-and-go."

Janet sighs. "I think it got-up-and-went." Betty gives her a quizzical look. "You know, like that old saying. Anyway, how're you, Betty? Still married?"

"Yes, 22 years to Jack. Almost too many to count."

"How *is* Jack?"

"Oh, he's good. You know he has MS, right? Doesn't get him down much. But it *does* keep him in a wheelchair most of the day."

Janet pivots. "Do you have kids?"

"No, never did. Never could. But then, being principal and all, I'm saddled with about 80 every year. Hands pretty full."

"Sounds like it."

"Hey, like I said, I sure enjoyed meeting Jonny. During the service, I noticed he has a fine voice. You know, I could sure use him in the choir."

"Oh, I can't imagine we'll be here that long. After I sell the house, well, I'm not sure what I'll do. But I *do need* to decide what to do with our house in St. Louis. It's a good market right now. And with my husband gone and Jonny off to college next year, I sure won't need the space."

Betty considers this. "Where *is* Jonny, anyway? I'd love to say hi."

"Oh. He's camped out in his bedroom. I think he's watching a Cardinals game. He spends a lot of time in there. I'm a little worried about him, to tell you the truth."

"Janet, hon, school started last week and I'd love to see him there if you decide to stay. I don't know if you heard, but this is Medicine Park's last semester. Starting January, we're consolidating with Elgin High till we can get a new school built. That's the idea, anyway."

Janet walks slowly to the couch and sits beside Betty. "I honestly don't know what our plans are." For the first time, she looks Betty directly in the eye. "Since Jonny and I returned from the funeral, I haven't been able to get out the front door. I feel paralyzed."

This startles Betty. "You don't mean that. *You?*"

"I can't get out of my robe, Betty. I can barely function." She fights back tears. "God, I'm a mess."

Betty squeezes Janet's hand. *"You poor dear! I can't imagine…burying a husband and both parents, back-to-back like that…"*

Janet's voice cracks. "Maybe if I could brush my teeth, that'd be a start…"

"Well, I'm great at that! I brush Jack's all the time, no matter how hard he fights." Betty jumps up and pulls Janet to her feet. "Let's get you to the bathroom and load up that toothbrush!"

Herman Lace has lived like a bachelor the past three months and, man, does it show! Books and newspapers and dishes and ashtrays are strewn around the living room of his creaky, fraying house. His daughter, Bren, who recently returned from Illinois, initially tried to straighten up behind him – a thankless job she quickly abandoned.

On this breezy mid-September evening, Herman sits in his well-worn armchair, reading Jack London's *Call of the Wild*. His attention, however, drifts across the room where Bren fingers the keys of her second-hand upright piano.

"Sounds nice, dear," Herman says in his most encouraging tone. "What is it?"

Bren stops and gives him an apologetic look. "Oh. Just a song I'm trying to finish. I'm not sure if it's any good."

Herman puts his book aside and shuffles to the piano. "Does it have words yet?"

"Uh…yeah. It's about a friend back in Benton. I started writing it on guitar…but I think it sounds better on piano."

"Will you sing it to me? I'd love to hear it."

Bren's not sure about this, but she decides to take the plunge. After a brief musical intro, she begins singing in a voice that's hesitant, yet engaging.

Look in the mirror, who do you see?
See yourself clearer, set yourself free
Addison, give us a look at you
Don't need to make up, no need to fake up
Tune out the blah, blah, blah on the phone…

Bren gathers confidence as she launches into the chorus.

Ooooh, trust how you feel, yeah, find what is real
Addison, the world is waiting for you
Addison, the world is waiting for you
Addison, the world is waiting for you.

She stops playing and turns to her dad. "There's another verse. I'm still working on it."

Herman smiles and gives her an affectionate pat on the shoulder. "That's beautiful, dear. Keep at it. You have talent!"

Bren blushes, but is obviously pleased. "Thank you, Dad." She decides to tell him how she feels in the moment. "You know, I like you a lot better when you're not drinking."

Herman is taken aback, but quickly recovers. "You're beginning to sound like your *mother*. But no one's perfect, I suppose." After a reflective pause, Herman adds, "All's forgiven if you'll come back to school."

Medicine Park High is a rambling timber and cobblestone building that resembles a frontier outpost during the 19th-century Indian Wars. The school, located on North Tackle Box Road, two miles east of Lake Lawtonka, is less than 60 yards from Park Baptist Church. To growing families in the area, it's practically one-stop shopping.

On this 22nd morning of October, Herman Lace's American History class is inordinately antsy. All 11 of them. Maybe it's the brisk fall weather. But you don't have to be seated in the front of the room to smell the booze oozing from Herman's pores.

It's only ten minutes until the noon bell, and he's already depleted the lion's share of a pint of Jim Beam, the bottle nestled inside a brown paper sack and haphazardly stuffed into the bottom drawer of his desk. And now, Herman hears the bottle insistently calling to him yet again.

Getting to his feet, he glances around the room, his eyes in the advanced stage of glazed-over. He decides to bring the period to a close. "Ladies and gents, I want you to read chapter six tonight. It's an analysis of the Supreme Court case of 'Brown vs. the Topeka Board of Education'." He stifles a belch. "In case you're wondering why that's important, imagine having Negroes and natives here with you in class. That's the gist of it." He glances around the room, trying to maintain his balance. "Questions?" A hand shoots up from the middle of the room. "Ah, Mr. Collins. Stand and grace us with your wisdom."

Dale Collins hesitantly rises to his feet. Sporting a crew cut, t-shirt, and letter jacket, he has obviously spent too much time in the locker room. "Mr. Lace, I always wondered what Whitefeather's doing here." He glances over at Blaze, who's slumped down in his chair a few feet away. "I mean, shouldn't he be at Fort Sill with the rest of 'em?"

Blaze shoots him a menacing glance. "*What the fuck, Collins?*"

Herman jumps in. "Watch your mouth, Blaze. Collins, Mr. Whitefeather is a legitimate and appreciated member of this class."

Collins protests. "The only reason he's here – his dad sucked up to the mayor."

What happened next is mostly a blur in Herman Lace's mind: He remembers seeing Whitefeather spring to his feet to confront Collins. But before they converge in fisticuffs, Jonny Sparks – charging from the back of the room – leaps onto Collin's back and rides him in circles like a bronco buster. Collins swings wildly as Blaze plows into his chest and knees him in the groin.

The next thing Herman remembers is standing at the door of Betty Allen's office, watching her scold the three pugilists seated across the desk from her. She then turns her attention to Herman as she leads him down the hallway.

"I'll sort this out myself, Mr. Lace." Betty snaps as she looks him up and down. "But the first order of business is *for you* to go home and stay away from here a few days. You need to think this whole thing over!"

"Whaddaya mean?" Herman says, confused.

"As of now, you're suspended. You reek of alcohol and you better straighten yourself out before you come back. *If you come back!*"

Herman is stunned. After 20 years, this is his first disciplinary trip to the principal's office. And he hates the feeling.

As Herman Lace is fond of saying, "Folks in Medicine Park have lived here all their lives but have no idea what goes on beneath the surface."

This is certainly true about the goings-on at the Sportsman's Club on the east bank of Lake Lawtonka, three miles north of town. It's the mayor's establishment, owned and operated. All three Comanche County commissioners feel Ben Thomas' ownership is a conflict of interest. They also know that the free-flowing liquor, rampant gambling, and onsite prostitution are blatantly illegal. Mayor Thomas, however, insists that the 93 acres the club is built on – and his family *lives on* – is incorporated land beyond the county's legal jurisdiction.

Rumors spread that the commissioners receive bribes from Medicine Park's flamboyant mayor. If true, the club's gambling operation probably funds them. Many speculate that most of the revenue comes from Army officers at neighboring Fort Sill, about eight miles south. Indeed, many nights you can see convoys of olive-drab vehicles exit highway 58 and wind along the long gravel road that leads to the gated entrance and parking lot beyond.

The clubhouse, built of cedar and stone, is at the end of a small peninsula that juts out to the lake. The facility provides no boating or fishing activities; it's for *indoor sports* only, and the tiny wood-hewn cabins adjacent to the clubhouse are primarily utilized as rent-by-the-hour love nests.

Inside, the club's large communal area features two large fireplaces at each end. An array of wall-mounted elk, moose, and bison heads stare out at customers seated at the central bar and adjacent dining booths.

The real action, however, takes place in the spacious, smoke-filled poker room in the back. Rodrigo, the omnipresent bouncer, ensures that no one enters without a pre-approved membership card – or are personally 'vouched for' by the mayor.

It's Saturday night in the poker room. Full house. Eager gamblers are scattered around the tables, looking to improve their fortunes. In the far corner, Mayor Ben Thomas stares wistfully at his cards as two Army officers and the town's football coach, Carter Singleton, await his bet.

"I call," the mayor says. His hesitant voice speaks loudly as he flips two twenties into the center pot. The phrase 'no guts, no glory' certainly applies to the cash-and-IOU only cost of doing business here.

"Okay, let's see 'em!" barks Colonel Turley, impatiently.

The mayor reluctantly turns over his cards to reveal a pair of Queens.

"Ha!" chortles Turley, throwing down three nines.

"Got *me*," says Captain Fredrickson, showing a pair of Jacks.

"Shit fire." Coach Singleton winces, tugging on the bill of his cap as he throws his cards face down on the table.

"Come on home." Turley chortles, raking in the pile of scratch from the middle of the table.

The captain wearily massages his temples. "I say we take a break."

"Drinks are on me!" Turley says, waving a fistful of newly-won bills in the air.

Mayor Ben Thomas and Coach Carter Singleton share drinks at a booth next to the main room's crowded bar. They struggle to hear each other over the raucous din.

"I should probably kill her," Carter says as he leans closer to the mayor.

Ben strains to hear. "*What?*"

"Betty. Betty Allen. I should take her out."

"Get over it, Carter. You're drunk."

"She's a pain in my ass."

"That's *your* problem. She's useful to me."

"You mean, that 55th anniversary bullshit?"

"There's an election coming up. She's helping me put a positive spin on things."

"People around here are broke! They're worried, Ben. She can't spin *that*. She can't stop the pill pushers and bootleggers from coming in, either."

"That's what our new sheriff's for. To clean that up."

"Well, he'd better start scrubbing." Carter snaps, compulsively pulling on his gold-plated championship ring.

Ben sips his whiskey sour. "Look, new schools and shopping centers are great diversions."

"You're so full of shit."

"Your problem, Carter. You talk too much."

Coach rolls his eyes. "And the mayor calls the kettle black."

"Just do your job." Ben snaps. "If you can't win more games next season, with *Elgin's* boys…"

"Oh, spare me."

"…then *you're* the one who's useless. Not Betty Allen."

50

It's Monday morning at Medicine Park High, and the only one missing from Herman Lace's American History class is Herman.

Coach Carter Singleton, sleeves rolled up, stands beside Lace's desk. He glances around the room with a weary look. "All right, everyone. Listen up. I'm subbing for Mr. Lace. For the time being. Seems he's under the weather."

The coach consults a page of hand-written instructions on his desk. "Okay. I see here, you're on Chapter 6. The Supreme Court." He hitches up his pants as he walks around the desk. "But first, a couple of announcements. Sparks? Jonny Sparks."

Jonny, seated in the left corner of the room, hesitantly raises his hand. The coach looks him up and down. "Ah, Mr. Sparks. The principal wants to see you in her office after class. I hope you're not in trouble, Ace. Don't want to get sideways with *her*."

Coach Carter now locks eyes with Blaze Whitefeather, seated in the back row, slumped down in his chair. "Whitefeather? Yeah, I'm talking to you, Chief. I wanna see you in *my office* immediately after school. Got that?"

Blaze reluctantly nods. The coach turns his attention back to the group. "Okay, now crack open those books and start reading. I don't care where. I just don't wanna hear a peep from you clowns. *Comprende?*"

Betty Allen sits at her desk, immersed in a pile of paperwork. There's a knock at her door. "Yes? Come in."

The door slowly swings open and Jonny Sparks pokes his head inside. Betty's glad to see him. "*Ah, Jonny*, please have a seat."

"Am I in trouble?" he asks, plopping down in the wooden chair across from her.

Betty laughs. "No, no. Hardly. I just wanna talk for a minute." She leans forward and gives Jonny a searching look. "How's your mother?"

"I guess she's okay. Some good days, some bad."

"I reckon so. Look, I plan to stop by for a visit soon. Will you tell her that?"

Jonny shrugs. "Yeah, sure."

"You know, from what I remember of your mom. Well, she was an inspiration. And I hope she can find a toehold here. I'd hate for a bright spirit like hers to go to waste." She tries to read Jonny's blank stare. "Do you have any idea what I'm talking about, hon?"

"Uh, not really."

"Well, maybe someday you will. Maybe if you start paying the *slightest bit of attention*." She decides to ease off. "I sense a lot of potential in you, Jon. That's all."

Jonny's uncomfortable with this conversation. "Maybe…I guess."

Betty wonders if she's getting through. She reaches into her top drawer and pulls out a sealed manila envelope. "Jon, I'm sending you on a mission. You have a car, right?"

"Yeah. Me and mom are sharing Grandpa's."

"Good. Do me a favor. Please take this package to Herman Lace. He's just north of the dam at East River Drive. Corner of Elm. The address is 115."

"I'll find it."

Jonny walks toward the school parking lot, clutching the envelope Principal Betty gave him. Up ahead, he sees three letter-jacket-clad classmates gathered around his burgundy and white '56 Chevy. He immediately recognizes Dale Collins.

"Hey," Jonny says, trying to sound nonchalant. "What's happening?"

"*You're* happening, Sparks. You're on my shit list."

"I'm flattered." Jonny flashes a fake smile as he eyes Dale's companions glaring at him. They aggressively puff cigarettes.

Dale steps closer to Jon. "No one jumps me, Sparks! Especially in class."

"I apologized already."

"That was in front of old lady Allen. *I want it to my face.*"

Jonny's distracted by the sound of a vehicle door opening a few yards away. All heads turn to see a hulking man, in gray coveralls, pull a chain saw from the back of a faded brown van and slam the door shut. He walks their way, then stops and appraises them.

"Any trouble here?"

"Uh, no," Dale says. "No trouble, Buddy. Just tellin' stories."

"Don't you have to be somewhere?" Buddy replies. Jonny can't take his eyes off the jagged, three-inch scar on his left cheek. There's an even larger one on his neck, below.

"Yeah," Dale replies. "We're takin' off. See ya."

Jonny watches Dale's pack hurriedly walk away, spooked by Buddy's presence.

"New around here?" Buddy says, checking Jonny out.

"Been here a couple weeks."

"Well, don't let those punks fuck with ya. They're dicks. Keep your head down, you'll be okay."

Jonny sizes him up, guessing he's at least 30. "You work here?"

"Yup. Janitor. Handyman. Jack of all trades. Today I'm a tree trimmer. Name's Buddy."

"Jonny. Jonny Sparks."

Jonny reaches out for a handshake, but Buddy has abruptly turned and started toward the schoolyard, the chainsaw slung over his shoulder.

Driving west on Tackle Box Road, Jonny glimpses the foothills of the Wichita Mountains on the far side of Lake Lawtonka. The roadway, snaking south toward town, melds into East Lake Drive.

With the creek on his right and Medicine Park's main drag lying ahead, Jonny can't shake the image of 'Chain Saw Buddy.' His thoughts, however, are rudely interrupted by the piercing blast of a police siren. Glancing in his rear-view mirror, he sees a spinning red light atop a black & white sedan.

"Shit!" Jonny says, pulling to the side of the road. "Now what?" Jonny fidgets, trying to stay cool as a burley officer, Sheriff Roy Smirk, taps on his window and signals for him to roll it down.

"Let's see your license, Son," the sheriff says, adjusting his reflective shades. Jonny fishes in his wallet, removes his I.D., and hands it to the officer, who scrutinizes it. "Hmm. St. Louis, Mizzou. You're a long way from home, slick."

"I've been meaning to get an Oklahoma license," Jonny replies, hoping the sheriff buys it.

"That so?" Sheriff Smirk leans back to appraise Jonny's car. "This a '56?"

"Yeah."

"How many miles on it?"

Jonny consults the odometer. "About 18 thousand."

"*What*?" Smirk replies, incredulously. "You shittin' me? My boy's been looking all over for one of these."

"It belonged to my grandpa," Jonny says, wondering why he was stopped. "Before he died."

"*Cherry*!" Smirk says with an admiring look. "You live in Medicine Park?"

"Yeah, with my mom. On Merry Circle."

"Merry Cherry," Smirk says with an annoying grin. "I'm new here myself. Mayor brought me up from Lawton." He hands the license back to Jonny. "Mind if I check the trunk?" Jonny holds out his keys, but the officer waves him off. "Step out. I want *you* to open it."

Jonny exits the car and ambles to the trunk. He opens it and stands back, ready for inspection. Nothing to see but a spare tire, car jack, and blanket.

"Lots of space back here," the officer says, peering inside and rummaging around. "My son does a lot of hunting. You hunt?"

"Uh, no."

"You could cram a whole goddamn moose in here!"

Smirk closes the trunk. "Okay, *a word to the wise*: I better not catch you with booze in there. Too many trouble-makers coming through town, trying to sell it. Jigs and injuns, mostly. You know it's illegal, right?"

"Yeah."

"This is a dry county. I aim to keep it that way."

"Yes, sir."

Smirk wipes his hands on his pants. "Okay, slick, get moving. And if you ever decide to let go of this baby, I want first crack. Got that?"

Jonny's police stop was just two blocks from Herman Lace's tiny, run-down house. Jonny turns left on Elm and pulls up in front. He spots Lace in the yard, watering a patch of faded pink zinnias. Jonny emerges from his car, special delivery in hand.

Herman's face lights up. "Mr. Sparks! What brings you to my prodigious estate?"

Jonny warily approaches Herman and hands him the envelope. "Mrs. Allen asked me to get this to you. Don't know what's in it."

"Well, well," Herman says, giving it a cursory glance. He starts to open it, then stops. "Why don't you join me on the porch for a civics lesson; got time?" Jonny nods and follows Herman up the front steps, entering his screened-in sanctuary. Herman invites Jonny to sit in a redwood rocker as he relights a cigar and slumps into a gray Adirondack next to him.

From Jonny's vantage point, he can see a swatch of the lake in the distance. But his attention is focused on Herman, who peruses the envelope's contents. "Just as I suspected," Herman mutters, holding up a batch of typed pages with red-penciled notes scrawled across them.

Herman shifts to his role as jaded lecturer. "Son, what you see here is a cold glimpse of the real world. Your principal asked me to ghostwrite a holiday supplement for the Gazette celebrating 55 years of joy and prosperity. Ha! All I'm trying to do is balance the ballyhoo with the facts. Most folks know this town's in the crapper." Herman takes a thoughtful puff on his cigar. "My point is, a historian is in service of the truth; a politician is in service of truth *management*."

Herman searches Jonny's face, hoping this sinks in. He decides to plow on. "Now, Sparks, I'm not saying Betty Allen's a politician. But *her boss* certainly is. And these ridiculous edits reflect his sentiments, not hers."

"Her boss?"

"Ben Thomas. The mayor, a one-man Chamber of Commerce. Betty's just going along to get along. And, I regret to say, me too. I'm sure you've sensed I'm in a bit of hot water. I hope this sordid assignment bails me out." He sighs and flashes Jonny a resigned smile. "That, lad, is how the world operates." After a moment of reflection, he turns back to Jonny. "Say, where's my manners? Can I get your something to drink?"

Before Jonny can answer, rousing pop music barrels onto the porch like a runaway train, gathering steam from the back of the house. Jonny cocks his head, his nervous system vibrating. It's an astonishing sound.

Herman chuckles. "My daughter Bren's playing the grooves off that record. Kinda catchy, huh? I'm starting to tolerate it."

Bren sits on her bed, acoustic guitar in hand, trying to emulate the chord progression playing on the portable record player on the corner nightstand. She looks up to see Jonny standing in the doorway. He mouths, "*Who is that?*"

Bren tosses her guitar on the bed, jumps up, and lifts the needle from the disc. "What!" she snaps, annoyed at the stranger interrupting a private moment.

"I've never heard that before."

Bren looks him up and down. "It's *She Loves You* by the Beatles."

"Put it back on!" Jonny says, eyeing the black cowboy boots below her knee-length red cotton dress.

"The minor chords are driving the melody," she replies, swiping the low-hanging bangs off her forehead.

Jonny's pumped up. "It's the *harmonies* that get *me!*"

"George told me it's #1 in England." She opens her top dresser drawer and rummages through it. "I've got a letter from him, somewhere."

Jonny can't hold back; he begins singing the chorus, shaking his head, side to side:

> "She loves you – yeah, yeah, yeah!
> She loves you – yeah, yeah, yeah!
> With a love like that, you know you should be glad..."

Bren whirls around to measure the source of this intriguing voice. He's good, she thinks. Who *is* this guy, anyway? And where'd he come from?

Coach Carter Singleton checks his watch. He removes the whistle hanging around his neck and shoves it into his top desk drawer. It's nearly 5:00 – an hour after school – and Blaze Whitefeather is a no-show. "Fuck that numbskull," Coach mutters under his breath.

He hears footsteps outside his office door. His assistant, Jake Marsh, pops in to report that the players have finished their mile run and are heading to the showers. "Good," Coach Singleton replies, walking to the window. He looks out to see a football player, in full pads, on his hands and knees, vomiting on the track.

"It's their last day of punishment," Marsh reminds him.

"Gotta make an example of 'em, Jake. The smokers and drinkers. You can't lose discipline and win games."

"Right. But there's no games left."

Coach turns to him. "Just because we don't have enough players to finish the season, Marsh, there's always next year. The younger guys gotta see what winning looks like. Or we're sunk."

"Seems you've got a visitor," Marsh says, pulling Blaze Whitefeather from the hall to the open doorway.

"That'll be all, Jake," Coach Singleton replies. "Get those jerseys in the wash and then lock up."

"Aye, aye, captain," Marsh salutes, rounding the corner.

The coach gives Whitefeather a calculating gander, then motions for him to take a seat in the chair across from his desk. The office feels cold and joyless. Spartan and gray. A large trophy dominates the room, perched on an adjacent metal filing cabinet.

"Here's a fun fact for you, Whitefeather," the coach says as he plops down in his chair. "In 1953, ten years ago next month, the Medicine Park Falcons won the Division 3 title with a 10 and 0 record." He makes a show of twirling his gaudy championship ring in front of Whitefeather. "This season, we didn't win a single fucking game. I can barely field a team. *What's changed?*"

Blaze shrugs. Coach rises from his chair and paces the room. "Tell me, Chief, know who quarterbacked that championship team back in '53?" He's not waiting for an answer. "Does Buddy Allen ring a bell?"

He now has Blaze's attention. "Buddy, the janitor?"

"*The same!*" Coach snatches the football lying on his desk and tosses it in the air. "Now, this one's gonna hit closer to home: Ten years ago, your father returned a war hero. A decorated fighter pilot. *Where's he today?* A goddamn ghost! A crop duster who came up empty – in every sense of the word."

"Hey!" Blaze snaps, squirming to keep from attacking Singleton.

"It's the hard truth, Son. See, glory's a fleeting thing. Guys like Buddy Allen and Sampson Whitefeather have failed imaginations. They never had a grasp of the world. Couldn't build on a dream."

Blaze jumps up and heads for the door.

"*Stop where you are!*" the coach yells. "Listen to me, Chief, or I'll run your ass out of here!" Blaze turns to face him. "Sit back down."

Blaze reluctantly returns to the chair. "Okay," coach continues. "Next season, you'll be a senior. We'll be together at Elgin High, and we'll have a shot at a great team. You're a hell of a runner, Son, best I've ever seen. And I'll tell ya, I'm *more than disappointed* you didn't play this year. I'm willing to forgive that, look past it. But I need you to get your fucking head on straight. You can graduate from a pretty good school and maybe get a scholarship. To be brutally honest, that's your only shot, 'cause you're far from the brightest bulb in the attic." He stops tossing the football and looks Blaze directly in the eye. "Is any of this getting through to you, Chief?"

Blaze can only return his icy glare.

Principal Betty Allen nears the end of her day. She glances at her watch, realizing she'll be late getting home and starting dinner. Her husband, Jack, is probably worrying about her. She decides to pack it in, stuffing a file folder into her purse and grabbing her coat.

There's a rap, rap, rap on her door. She knows the sound. "What is it, Carter?" she responds, warily.

Coach Singleton steps into her office. He's wearing his usual letter jacket and ball cap. He needs a shave, Betty thinks. "Got a minute?" Carter asks.

Betty forces a smile. "Always for you, coach."

"I'm just wondering, how much longer do I have to fill in for Lace? Cause I know bupkis about history. And to be honest, I don't have the time."

"Gym classes overwhelming you?" Betty replies, forcing a smile. Coach doesn't appreciate her sarcasm. "Look, Carter, Herman's coming back next week. Surely you can hold on till then."

"Betty, this year's a disaster. But come January, at Elgin, well, it looks a whole lot better. *For me*, anyway. But what about you? Elgin has a good principal. And the mayor plans to keep him."

"Ben's promised me a job on his staff. Until the new school's built."

"Jesus, Betty, he's not building a new school. Surely, you know that! He's building a racetrack on that land he annexed. He's getting into the quarter horse business. Among other things."

Betty considers this. "I don't believe you."

"He told me himself." Coach Singleton watches her, intently, as she starts putting on her coat. His eyes fix on her large breasts, protruding beneath her tight silk top. His gaze slides down to her hips as she wiggles into her wrap. "You sure know how to get me started." He winks.

"I didn't hear that," she replies in her chilliest tone.

"*Sure you did.*"

"You're blocking the door."

"Betty…look at me. You can't keep pretending we never happened."

This disturbs Betty. "You better go, Carter. *Now.*"

Frustrated, Singleton rushes out, practically knocking over the hulking janitor mopping the floor outside her office. "Move it, Allen!" the coach says, darting quickly down the hallway.

Buddy watches him go, then pokes his head through the door to check on the principal. "Everything okay, sis?"

The sun is disappearing on the horizon, casting a late-autumn glow on Herman Lace's front porch. Bren and Jonny sit together, laughing, as Bren rolls a cigarette from her tobacco pouch.

Jonny takes a swig from his Coke bottle. "I can't believe you spent the summer in – where'd you say, Benton?"

"Right. Illinois."

"That can't be too far from St. Louis."

"About 100 miles, I think," Bren says, firing up a smoke. "In fact, me and my friend Patty drove there one weekend to see James Brown—"

"*You saw James Brown?* Me too—"

"At the Opera House. In July. Right after the fourth."

"You've gotta be kidding," Jonny says. "I think I was there that same night! Marvin Gaye opened for him, right?"

"Right! And the Drifters."

"And Ruby and the Romantics."

"Yes!" Bren replies, handing Jonny one of her cigarettes. "I can't believe you were there! What're the odds on that?"

"I thought he'd *never come on stage*. But when he did, man, what a voice! I wish I could sing like that!"

"*No one can*. But you've got a good one, Jonny."

"I was in a band for a while. We did a lot of Buddy Holly stuff. And Roy Orbison."

"God, I love Roy Orbison! We should work up one of his songs."

"Has to be *Only the Lonely*, that's his best."

"You play an instrument?"

"Electric bass. But it's back in St. Louis." Jonny thinks on this. "*I wish I was back in St. Louis...*"

"Yeah, I'd love to blow outta here, too. I'm moving to Dallas next spring – to live with my cousin." She takes a deep drag and exhales. "Anything to get away from my dad."

"He's not so bad."

"Maybe. All I know, my mother's worse."

Jonny nods, knowingly. "That's *another* thing we have in common."

"What's that?"

"Mom problems."

When Jonny returns to the house on Merry Circle Drive, his mother is talking on the wall phone in the kitchen. She hears Jonny in the living room and abruptly brings the conversion to a close.

"What's up, Mom?" Jonny calls out, heading for his room.

"I just got off the phone with Betty Allen," Janet replies. "She invited us to church this Sunday."

Jonny's curiosity wins the day and he takes a detour back to the kitchen. "What'd you tell her?"

"I told her I didn't have anything to wear." Jonny looks her over. She's in a pale house dress and flats – an improvement over the past weeks of bathrobe-only. "Most of my clothes are still in St. Louis."

"You have *something*. You wore a nice dress at the funeral."

"You brought a sport coat, didn't you?" Janet replies. "I kept a few of your grandfather's ties." Janet sniffs the air and frowns. "Have you been smoking?"

Jonny deflects. "No way I'm going to church."

Janet pulls a can of Green Giant asparagus from the overhead cupboard. "You know, Jon, I'm thinking about going back to Missouri, maybe get a job at the Dispatch while I still know people. How's that sound?" Jonny shrugs. His ambivalence surprises her and she gives him a searching look. "I thought you were chomping at the bit to leave here."

"It's not so bad, for now. At least I finally met someone I can talk to."

"Oh? Who's that?"

"Just someone. Someone pretty cool."

Buddy Allen's ramshackle farmhouse, four miles east of town, screams, "Junkyard dog." His neighbors heartily concur. The collection of abandoned, rusted-out cars in his front yard are either on concrete blocks or simply stripped and tireless; all are engulfed by weeds. Buddy calls it his sculpture garden. His wife calls it an eyesore.

Tonight, like most nights, Buddy stands inside the deteriorating shed behind his house, attempting to build something resembling furniture with his bench saw, hand planer, and power drill. By now, he's so tipsy on Pabst Blue Ribbon he's simply venting his anger on blocks of wood.

Tonight, unlike most nights, his wife, Carla, is determined to make good on her long-promised exit from the junkyard. She's packed two suitcases and they await her at the front door. All that's left is a sad walk to the shed and a final goodbye.

Standing in the dark, a few yards from the shed's open door, she watches Buddy plod under a work light hanging from the ceiling. She doesn't blame him for everything. She thinks about all those years he suffered in prison. She recalls her own pain, shame, and loneliness. To her surprise, in this moment, she feels as sorry for him as she does for herself.

The Medicine Park Baptist Church was dedicated in 1929, two days before the stock market crash that sent the nation's economy tumbling. Since that time, the town's fortunes ebbed and flowed, but the Church remained upright throughout.

Today's Sunday attendance is far short of the 70-plus seating capacity inside the sanctuary. Jonny and Janet Sparks sit together in a near-empty pew in the back of the house. Jonny surveys the room every few minutes, hoping to get a glimpse of Bren Lace. But he knows he's kidding himself. Janet tries to stay focused on Pastor Roberts, who delivers the closing benediction. Cue the choir, rising in unison to sing *A Mighty Fortress Is Our God*. Betty Allen stands in front of them, conducting. She turns unexpectedly to search the congregation, making eye contact with Janet. Janet returns Betty's reassuring smile as Betty turns back to the choir, waving her arms to bring the vocals to a crescendo. Jonny notes that the paltry group in burgundy robes could certainly use his voice.

After the service, attendees gather outdoors in the rear courtyard, adjacent to the gravel parking lot. The rose bushes are bare this late October afternoon, but the newly planted Violas and Chrysanthemums add a welcome dash of color to the post-event socializing.

Jonny's surprised when, seemingly out of nowhere, Coach Singleton approaches him and his mother. Coach introduces his wife, Rita. Janet remembers Singleton from high school and dons a friendly face. As she makes small talk with Carter, she notes that Rita wears too much make-up and her short skirt is embarrassingly immodest.

Jonny suddenly remembers he has the keys to the Chevy, excuses himself, and heads to their car to listen to the radio. He can usually tune-in WKY in Oklahoma City, which dependably plays the hits. Walking through the lot, he sees Betty Allen struggling to move her husband, Jack, from his wheel chair to the passenger seat of their white Oldsmobile. Jonny stops to lend a hand, knowing a suck-up to Principal Betty can pay dividends. He smiles to himself, realizing Herman Lace's lecture about the 'real world' is already sinking in.

Inside his car, Jonny sings along with the Four Season's *Walk Like a Man*. Through the front windshield he sees Coach Singleton approach Betty, who stands in front of her open trunk, placing Jack's wheelchair inside. The coach grabs Betty's arm and pulls her away from the car. She's both alarmed and annoyed. "*What're you doing?*"

"Just hear me out, Betty!" he pleads. "I think I deserve that."

"This isn't the time or place, Carter," she says, glancing around, self-consciously.

"Why won't you see me, Betty? You keep avoiding me."

"*Because we're over.*"

Carter feels increasingly frustrated. "If I can't have you, Betty, *no one* can. Not your decrepit husband, not Ben Thomas, not Janet Sparks."

"What're you talking about?"

"I see how you look at her." He snaps, pulling her further away from her car.

"Are you insane?"

"I know you love me. You said so! Remember?"

She pulls her arm from his grasp. "I was flattered, Carter. *Needy*...I'll admit that, but it sure wasn't love."

"Just say the word and I'll leave Rita."

"Nobody's leaving anybody!"

"What about our weekend in Wichita Falls—"

"That's enough, Carter!"

"How it felt to hold each other...Jesus, Betty, you sucked my dick!"

"Shush your mouth! *That'll never happen again,* I assure you."

"It was real, Betty. I know you felt it."

"It was a huge mistake, Carter. And every day, I pray for forgiveness."

Coach Singleton is consumed with his desire for her. "*You* pray for forgiveness? Well, I pray too, Betty. *I pray to God your husband doesn't find out about us...*'cause that would ruin everything, wouldn't it?"

Alarmed, Betty rushes to her car door, slides behind the wheel and starts the engine. Coach Singleton, standing beside the Olds, angrily kicks up a patch of gravel. He watches, hands on his hips, as she drives away.

Jonny, still gazing through the windshield of his Chevy, wonders what in hell he just witnessed. He makes a mental note: this place is a lot weirder than it seems.

Back home, even before Jonny wrestles out of his church clothes, he gets on the phone and calls the Lace residence, hoping Bren answers instead of her father. He's in luck!

"Bren? Hi, it's Jonny."

"Oh, hi!" she replies. "How was church?"

"*Just church*." He pauses for a moment. "I'd, uh, like to see you. You busy this afternoon?"

"Yeah, sort of." Jonny can practically hear his own disappointment. But then: "I'm meeting up with some friends. Like to take me?"

"Sure, where?"

"Come by in an hour. You'll find out."

She constantly keeps Jonny off-balance. Surprisingly, he likes it. And he hopes his mom doesn't plan to use the car.

Bren tells Jonny to turn off highway 58 onto McIntosh Road. They head east, with Lake Lawtonka now in the rearview mirror. Bren grabs the American Spirit rolling papers from the dashboard and raids her tobacco pouch. Jonny's eyes stray from the road as he appraises the Spirit-package logo, with the image of an Indian chief in full headdress, smoking a peace pipe. He wonders what Blaze Whitefeather would think of the artwork. Perhaps he'll soon find out.

Jonny's surprised when he encounters the vast expanse of land occupied by the Whitefeather family. Several structures, large and small, punctuate the rolling 48-acres of tallgrass, sage, oak and dogwood trees. A two-story clapboard house and lofty barn are gateways to nearby gardens, horse stables, tipi clusters, and landing field.

Bren instructs Jonny to drive past the house and park in front of Sampson Whitefeather's former aircraft maintenance shop – more of an overgrown shed, really, haphazardly constructed of pinewood and corrugated tin. Bren reaches over to the steering wheel and pushes the car horn. After a few beeps, Blaze Whitefeather emerges from the screened front door. He motions for Bren and Jonny to join him inside.

The shed's interior is in the final stages of a radical transformation. Workbenches and tool cabinets and metal-working equipment have been replaced by guitar stands, keyboards, microphones, and amplifiers. A Ludwig drum kit is set up in the corner. The walls are padded. So is the ceiling. Jonny glances around, amazed at what looks like a budding rehearsal room.

Bren escorts a gregarious stranger toward Jonny and introduces him. "Jonny, this is Parker Tate. We have some classes together at Elgin." Jonny grips Tate's extended right hand, gazing at what appears to be the reincarnation of Buddy Holly – a tall, gangly lad with black horn-rimmed glasses and a trim, pompadour hairdo.

"I've heard a lot about you," Parker says. "Bren tells me you can really sing."

"Yeah?" Jonny replies. "I'm surprised because she doesn't tell me *anything.*"

Inside Jonny's car, heading for home, Jonny gives Bren the silent treatment. He's not sure why, but he's hurt.

Bren has finally had enough. "What's with you, anyway? You treated Parker like crap. He was nice to you!"

Jonny explodes. "I can't believe you're going to school in Elgin! Thanks, Bren, for telling me." His tone is laced with sarcasm. "I thought you were Medicine High's most beautiful dropout."

"Look, Jonny, what can I say? There's no way I could go back there."

Jonny's totally confused. "*Why?* Is it your dad?"

Bren stares straight ahead as Jonny anxiously taps on the steering wheel. Bren decides to push on. "I wanted to give Elgin a shot. Turns out, I kinda like it."

"The school, or Parker Tate?"

"*Yeah,* I like Parker. He's a nice guy, a *talented* guy. And he wants to *be* somebody."

"Oh, and I'm not rich enough for you, can't buy you guitars and amps like him? Is that it?"

Bren turns to Jonny. "Listen, a door opened up for me. Who knows, it may never happen again. But I'm walking through it. *I'm running through it!*" Bren searches Jonny's face, hoping this sinks in. "Will you come with me?"

Jonny stares back at Bren, wondering if he can trust her.

The Medicine Park Sheriff's Office is smack dab in the center of town, up the street from the volunteer Fire Department. It's tucked inside the rustic redwood Civic Center, which also houses the local license and tax agencies – all connected by a central corridor populated by a wooden bench, rusted brochure stand and temperamental water fountain.

Inside the Sheriff's Office, Officer Roy Smirk sits at his desk, gripping a coffee mug and reading the Gazette. A large Comanche County map dominates the wall behind him. Colored pushpins highlight areas around Medicine Park, as well as westerly positions near Founder's Lake and the Wichita Mountains Wildlife Refuge. The sheriff's desk is flanked by an American flag on the left and an Oklahoma state flag on the right.

Smirk's deputy, Josh Waggoner, raps on the door, then pokes his head inside. "Excuse me, sheriff, a lady's out here to see you."

"Oh?" Smirk replies, sipping his coffee. "Who?"

"Rita Singleton." The sheriff gives him a blank stare. "Coach Singleton's wife."

"Oh! Send her in." Smirk tosses his paper to the corner of his desk. He gets up and greets Rita, who enters dressed more for a night of dancing than a Tuesday morning trip to town. "Sit down, hon," he says, indicating the metal folding chair nearest his desk. "What can I do you for?"

"May I smoke?" Rita asks, already pulling a pack of Marlboros from her purse.

"Sure, sure. Help yourself." Smirk waits for her to fire up. "I'd offer you a light, but I'm on the wagon." He tries to avoid looking up her short orange skirt.

"I'm here about my husband. Carter Singleton."

"Ah, yes, the coach. What about him?"

"He's disappeared. And I'm worried."

"Wait, wait, hold on a sec. Let's back up. When did you last see him?"

"Sunday night. He said he was going out, and never came back."

"And you waited *this long* to report him missing?"

"Well, yes." She crosses her legs and Smirk fights to maintain his concentration. "He's done this before. Run off for a couple days. But this time, it feels different."

"Whaddaya mean, run off?"

"Gone on a bender. Shacked up. I'm not gonna lie to ya. He's who he is. I've learned to live with it." She takes a deep drag off her cigarette. "But like I said, this time feels different."

"Why so?"

"He always leaves a note, an 'I'm sorry, I gotta split, remember I love you' sort of thing. This time, no note. I think he meant to come back."

"Where's he supposed to be today?"

"At school. But I called the principal's office and he wasn't there Monday, either."

Smirk considers this. "Okay…Rita, that's your name?" She nods, smokes. He searches his lower desk drawer and fumbles for a form. "Here…take this…it's a Missing Person's Report. Fill it out. Let's give him a couple days before we sound the alarm. In the meantime, I'll ask around. See what I can see. *And* if anything develops on your end, pick up the phone." He takes one last glance at her exposed thighs. "Sound like a plan?"

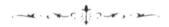

It's early Friday evening. Janet Sparks emerges from her kitchen, holding a 9-cup coffee percolator. Betty Allen, sitting in the dining room, takes a dainty bite of chocolate cake. "This is delicious, hon. You shouldn't have!"

Janet pours steaming brew into Betty Allen's porcelain cup. "It's a thank-you for all you've done." Betty blushes. "I mean it. You've been so kind to me. Everyone has, actually."

"Well, we love you. We hope you'll stay longer." She sips her coffee. "Umm. Tastes as good as it smells."

Janet chuckles. "You've been watching too many Maxwell House commercials."

"Pardon?"

"Never mind."

"Where's Jonny tonight?"

"At a party. In Elgin. Parker someone. Pate, or Tate. Jon took Bren Lace."

"*Oh, she's a hand full.* Her father, too."

"That's what I hear. Is he back in class?"

"Back this week. And seems to be on good behavior. *So far.*"

"Did Carter Singleton ever turn up?"

Betty shakes her head as she takes another sip. "No one's seen him."

Janet fumbles with her coffee cup. "Betty, can I ask you a personal question?"

"Sure, hon. What?"

"How are you and Jack doing? Does it ever get you down?"

"Oh, don't worry about us. We're fine."

"*I know it must be hard.*"

Betty reaches across the table, grabs Janet's hand, and squeezes it. "Honey, I've seen Jack go from complaining of aches and pains to a cane, then a wheelchair. That's how the disease marches. I just trust in the Lord. I have faith in all things."

"Really? Because after losing my husband, my whole family, for no conceivable reason, well, I have a hard time believing. In God, I mean."

"Janet, don't say that! Times like these are when we need him most."

The exclusive Tate home, three miles north of Elgin, was listed as a "mansion" by local realtors when it went on the market in 1960. That's when Wilton Tate, the biggest rancher east of Amarillo, purchased the 155-acre property. With cash. Tate quickly added an Olympic-sized swimming pool and rifle range, both near the newly-constructed quarter horse breeding and training facilities.

Tonight, local teens and young adults gather at Tate Manor to celebrate Wilton's social trek to Ft. Worth, leaving the estate in care of his sons, Parker and Tyson. The Tate brothers are as different as two siblings can be. Parker, the younger, is gregarious and rebellious. Tyson, eleven years his senior, is thoughtful and sincere. One is an aspiring pop star; the other is a 1st Lieutenant in the U.S. Army – a Special Forces Green Beret.

From the outside, Tate Manor is jaw-dropping. The 9,300 square-foot, two-story home is a fortress of pinewood, glass and bluff stone. Inside, the focal point of the central, first-floor living space is a crystal chandelier that dangles from the 25-foot vaulted ceiling. The entire east end is dominated by a fieldstone wall and fireplace. Near the entryway, a spiral staircase leads to the upstairs bed, bath, utility rooms, and spacious business office.

The first floor gathering space is so vast, it engulfs the evening's 50-plus partygoers – half who've dispersed to adjacent rooms for sidebar reveling.

Jonny and Bren huddle in a corner of the expansive kitchen, watching guests come and go from the living room, refreshing their drinks and diving into the chips, dips and pizza slices on the island countertop.

"Who're they?" Jonny whispers, indicating the quartet clustered in front of the open refrigerator.

"New classmates. Not exactly my best friends."

"No? What a surprise," Jonny teases. Bren pokes him with her elbow.

Jonny directs Bren's attention to the living room, visible from the open kitchen door. "What's up with Blaze and the mystery guy in there?" Blaze, seated on a sofa, converses intimately with a boyish, delicate-looking admirer. Blaze brushes his cheek with the back of his hand.

"I dunno," she shrugs. "Just friends. I think. You never know with Blaze."

"Not sure what that means…"

Bren's eyes light up as she looks across the room. "Here comes Parker, be nice." Parker Tate, in tight blue jeans and blousy silk shirt, approaches them.

"Hi, Parker!" Bren waves, gesturing him nearer. "Great party."

Parker joins them in the corner. "Thanks. Hey, I wanna introduce you to my big brother." He whistles into the living room and motions for Tyson to join them. A slender, earnest-looking fellow, appearing to be in his late twenties, crosses into the kitchen.

"Bren, Jonny, this is my brother, Tyson. He's just back from Vietnam, making the world safe for democracy."

"That's *Lieutenant* to you, punk," he replies, winking at Parker. Crew-cut Tyson, in slacks and polo shirt, aggressively pumps Jonny's hand.

Jonny tries to seem engaged. "Vietnam? What's happening there, anyway?"

"Jesus, don't get him started!" Parker groans.

Tyson jumps at this. "It's a mad house, man. A shit storm! The brass says we're winning, but I don't see it on the ground. I don't even know what we're fighting for!"

"That's what my dad says," Bren replies.

Their conversation's interrupted by the arrival of a beautiful, elegantly-dressed black woman. She appears to be near Tyson's age, but with greater poise.

"May I join this hen house?" she says with a warm smile.

"Sure, jump right in," Tyson replies. He turns to Bren and Jonny. "Kids…meet my wife, Melinda."

Melinda extends her hand to them. "Do you two have names?"

"I'm Jonny. This is Bren." Jonny's surprised to encounter a mixed-race couple in the Elgin outback. Or *anywhere* in Oklahoma, for that matter.

Melinda turns to Parker. "Is this the Bren you've been talking about?"

"The very one! And Jonny, here, is a helluva singer, maybe our newest band member." He turns and shouts toward the living room, "Whitefeather, get your ass in here!"

Jonny's unsure how to respond to Parker. He decides to be playful. "I'm taking a survey," Jonny says to the group. "Who here thinks Parker looks like Buddy Holly?"

"I do!" Melinda chimes in. "*Glasses and all.*"

Parker fondles his angular black rims. "Well, I *sound* like him, that's for sure." He turns to Blaze, who's just arrived from the living room. "Whitefeather, gimme a Holly back beat, will ya?"

Blaze begins pounding the kitchen counter with his palms, creating a driving, rhythmic pulse for Parker, who begins singing Buddy Holly's *Everyday*:

"Everyday – it's-a getting closer,
Going faster than a roller coaster,
Love like yours will surely come my way – hey, a-hey, hey
Everyday – it's-a getting faster,
Everyone says go ahead and ask her,
Love like yours will surely come my way – hey, a-hey, hey…"

Jonny joins in, harmonizing with Parker:

"Everyday seems a little longer,
Every way, love's a little stronger,
Come what may, do you ever long for
True love from me?"

Now Bren adds her voice to the chorus:

"Everyday – it's-a getting closer,
Going faster than a roller coaster,
Love like yours will surely come my way – hey, a-hey, hey!"

As their three voices intertwine, Blaze's pounding brings the song to a crescendo. They all laugh at the rousing burst of spontaneity. Melinda is delighted. "You all sound so good! *You should make a record.*"

"We need our own songs," Parker says. "That's where Bren comes in. She has some terrific ones, right, baby?"

"Maybe." Bren shrugs, modestly.

"Maybe, Baby." Jonny laughs. "It's definitely Buddy Holly night, and now, I'm privileged to know *two Buddies.*"

"Two?" Parker replies.

"Yeah. You, and the janitor at my school. Buddy Allen."

The remark meets with cold silence. Jonny looks around, wondering what he said to put such a sudden freeze on the festivities.

Melinda breaks the ice. "Buddy Allen killed my brother."

"He *what?*" Jonny can't believe what he just heard.

Melinda tries to smile, but can't. "He stabbed him in the throat. To death."

Mayor Ben Thomas's family residence is only a hop, skip, and jump north of the Sportsman's Club on the east bank of Lake Lawtonka. The house, protected by a formidable iron gate and surrounding cobblestone walls, is part of the expansive property originally owned by Ben's grandfather, Medicine Park founder JWE Thomas.

This early morning in late October, Sheriff Roy Smirk is at the gate, sitting inside his police black & white, awaiting clearance so he can drive to the front entrance. Once there, he'll wait even longer before a maid instructs him to "pull around back to the game house."

The rear brick & mortar building is a small replica of the main residence. When officer Smirk enters, he expects to see items like a billiard table, dartboard and pinball machine. Instead, it's a space more suitable for a Great White Hunter than a small-town mayor.

"Come in, sheriff!" Ben calls out from across the room, unzipping his olive-drab field jacket and casting it aside. "Starting to warm up out there!"

Smirk glances around, his eyes fixed on an array of weapons mounted on the far wall. "Whaddaya think of my collection?" Ben says, indicating the shotguns, single-shot and automatic rifles on display.

"Looks like you're ready for bear," Smirk replies, hitching up his khaki pants.

"Ready for just about anything!"

The sheriff's focus now turns to a severed whitetail deer's head, wrapped in a bloody cloth, lying on a nearby cleaning table.

"Oh, the buck," Ben smiles, proudly. "Huge sucker, huh? 10-point! Wandered onto the property last week and I finally bagged him. Boom! One shot with my Remington Seven. I'm in the middle of caping for the taxidermist. Can't have too many trophies, right?"

"Don't suppose," Smirk replies, caressing his badge.

"What's on your mind, officer?"

"Trying to get a line on Carter Singleton."

"Ah, yes. Our esteemed football coach. What gives?"

The sheriff is nearly transfixed by the deer's glassy eyes. "I uh, know he hangs out at the Sportsman's Club, I wonder if you or any of your people have seen him. You know, since he went missing. I didn't wanna poke around there without checking with you first."

"I appreciate that. No, Rodrigo tells me he hasn't been around for well over a week. Which is unusual. What's his wife say? Rita."

"Nothing new. Still hasn't heard from him."

"*I don't trust her.*"

"Me neither, to tell ya the truth."

The mayor walks over to the dead buck, holds it aloft by its antlers, and inspects it. "Why don't you stake out the house for a day or two? Watch the comings and goings. I don't think you need a warrant, maybe when she steps out, you can slip inside. Rummage around a bit." He carefully lays the bloody deer head back on the table.

"Alright, I'll doer," Smirk replies, thinking better of it.

"Oh, also try 'n' find out if Singleton has an insurance policy."

This surprises Smirk. "You think he could be dead?"

"Dunno. But if there's foul play, it'd certainly be a motive." The mayor picks up a nearby scalpel knife as he turns to face Smirk. "Anything else?"

Smirk hesitates. "I'm, uh, wondering if we should cast a wider net. Reach out to the County for help."

"No, no. It's best to keep this local. In the family. For the time being, anyway."

"Okay. You're the boss."

The mayor motions toward his collection of weapons on the back wall. "You know, Smirk, you're welcome to any of these guns. If or when the time comes."

It's 6:00 PM on Halloween eve and nearly dark.

Janet Sparks stands at her dining room table, shoveling an assortment of bite-sized candy bars into a plastic jack-o'-lantern, wondering if she'll get a single trick or treater. She decides to walk up and down the street, scouting for customers, carrying the candy with her.

Merry Circle Drive seems deserted. She considers trekking the two short blocks to Betty Allen's house, but she can't think of a good reason why. Except she wants to.

The locals refer to Lake Elmer Thomas as Founder's Lake.

The reservoir, spanning 475 acres, and with a maximum depth of 71 feet, is nestled south of town between the Wichita Mountains and the Fort Sill military base. Founder's Lake is the smaller sibling of neighboring Lawtonka, and it teems with channel cat and largemouth bass. Most are homegrown by the nearby Oklahoma Department of Wildlife hatchery.

November 1st kicks off *rainbow trout season* in Comanche County, but the hatchery only stocks the stream that flows south from Lake Lawtonka, through the dam spillway, into Gondola Pond and Medicine Creek. And the tourists are spilling in to nab them.

That's why, on this unseasonably warm Halloween night, Blaze Whitefeather, Jonny Sparks and Bren Lace are boating on Founder's Lake, which is nearly deserted and perfect for star-gazing. Before launching Blaze's 14-foot Alumacraft fishing boat from the ramp, the trio loads backpacks and paddles into the hull. Together, they guide the vessel into the water, hopping aboard as it drifts away from shore.

Janet, jack-o'-lantern in hand, stands on a dark street corner 15 yards from Betty's house. She clandestinely watches Betty, visible from the side kitchen window, washing dishes.

What's Betty thinking? she wonders. Does she wish she could fly away, escape from all this? Janet whispers, "Betty, you've never been *anywhere* and you cling so tightly to old beliefs! And yet, you're so generous. And loving. You're always full of hope."

At that moment, alone in the dark, Janet promises herself that she'll try her best not to judge Betty – ever again – as difficult as it may be.

It's an idyllic evening on Founder's Lake.

Tonight, both Jupiter and Saturn appear above the newly waxing moon, glowing faint orange and a mere sliver in the southwestern sky. Thousands of stars are in view, wowing the audience of three inside Blaze Whitefeather's fishing boat.

Blaze pulls a thermos from his backpack and vigorously shakes its contents. "I boiled 60 grams of powder. It tastes kinda like tea. But real bitter. So be prepared."

"Tell us more, Professor Peyote Button," Bren teases.

Blaze ignores her. "We split it three ways. Exactly. Drink too much, and someone's freaking out."

"What's this stuff supposed to do?" Jonny asks, grabbing cups from the backpack.

"Helps you see things you've never seen before." While Bren holds a flashlight, Blaze takes one of the cups from Jonny and pours. "And it feels like you're merging with everything. One spirit."

Bren jumps in. "Except for you, Blaze. You're *two*-spirit."

"That's true."

"What're you talking about?" Jonny says as Blaze hands Bren a full cup.

"In our tribe, two-spirit's a third way. A third gender." Jonny looks confused. "I've accepted that's who I am, my male side's merging with a female one. They slide, back 'n' forth. To avoid fighting each other."

"A wrestling match!" Bren chuckles.

Blaze shrugs. "I guess. I think it's part of the Great Mystery."

"To the Great Mystery!" Bren raises her cup. "Cheers!"

She chugs her psychedelic brew. Blaze follows. Jonny hesitates, then takes the plunge. "How long does this last?" Jonny asks, grimacing at the taste.

"Depends," Blaze replies. "Could be hours."

"*Hours*? You're shitting me!"

As Janet returns to her house, Halloween candy in tow, she's surprised to see a dozen or so small figures standing in the shadows near her front porch.

Kids, she thinks, moving closer get a better look. It's dark and she can't quite make out their shapes. Similar shapes. Matching costumes, perhaps. As she gets nearer, she realizes they seem more like large birds than children. The leader of the pack, on spindly legs, hops up to her.

"...Cranes!" Janet gasps. "I'll be damned!"

The sound of her voice sends the flock skyward, revealing their expansive wingspans as they soar. But the bold bird who approached Janet remains stubbornly grounded, fiercely locking eyes with her. It emits a sharp, vibrating trill.

"What a call you have!"

Another shrill whoop from the crane.

"What're you trying to tell me? Hmm? Are you lost?"

The crane begins hopping up and down, circling her.

Janet's perplexed. "I can't help you, silly bird. Whatever it is you want."

The crane, once again facing her, belts out another plaintive trill.

"I told you darling, I can't help you. *And I know you can't help me.*"

The insistent bird begins flapping its large white wings – and with a final, searching look at Janet, soars into the sky, heading south in the direction of the flock.

Janet tracks the crane as it disappears into the night. *What the hell was that?* she wonders. She's suddenly overwhelmed by a powerful sense of recognition. Her body starts to tremble and her eyes fill with tears.

"My God." She gasps, feeling the inexplicable, bittersweet presence of her mother.

Back on Founder's Lake, Blaze, Bren, and Jonny lie on their backs inside the boat, eyes fixed on the star-filled sky.

"Look!" Blaze calls out, urgently. "Off to the right, a flock of cranes."

"What?" Jonny replies.

Blaze sits up. "Whooping cranes. Migrating from Canada, on their way to the gulf."

Jonny searches the sky. "I don't see anything…"

Bren laughs. "Blaze, you're hallucinating!"

"Definitely." Blaze motions across the sky. "Check out the stars, all the colors."

"Check out *my* colors!" Bren says, waving her arms in front of her. "I'm making rainbows."

Blaze points to a thick cluster of stars overhead. "Look, now they're swirling!"

"Mine are *dancing*!" Jonny replies in amazement.

"We need music," Bren says, rummaging through the backpack. She pulls out a transistor radio, turns it on, and twists the dial, finding the song '*He's So Fine*' by the Chiffons.

Bren, sitting behind Jonny in the middle of the boat, jumps to her feet and pulls Jonny to his. They dance together, frenetically, and the Alumacraft sways side to side. Blaze yells, "Hey, you're rocking the boat!"

Jonny spins around, laughing, and shoots Blaze the finger. "Look who's talking, Whitefeather, you're king of the boat-rockers!" He suddenly loses his balance, slips, and falls forward, hitting the side of his head on the rim of the hull. Woozy, he staggers to his feet, wobbles back and forth – then tumbles overboard, splashing into the frigid water.

"Oh my God!" Bren cries out. "Help him, Blaze!"

Blaze, frozen for a moment, struggles to his feet. He hesitates, then plunges into the lake. Bren leans over the side of the craft, holding a flashlight, desperately hoping to catch a glimpse of either Blaze or Jonny – but the pool's dark surface is disturbingly still.

Jonny slowly sinks toward the bottom of the lake. His brain's limbic survival system senses an impending cold deathtrap. He struggles to maintain consciousness, unlocking a primal memory of his mother holding him tight against her bosom.

Lifesaving warmth suddenly arrives as he's wrapped in an underwater bear hug. Jonny's central cortex screams, "It's Blaze!" He instinctively clutches him around the neck. Pressed tightly against Blaze's chest, Jonny can now feel the warmth of Blaze's body and the rapid pounding of his heart. The pulsations surge through Jonny, its aortic rhythms throbbing in his inner ear.

Jonny experiences an amazing metamorphosis, his senses transforming into a giant, sentient red blood cell, swimming through Blaze's bloodstream. He's accompanied by a million others, like spawning salmon, rushing through a coronary artery on the way to Blaze's heart.

The heart-pounding 'thud-thud-thud' intensifies like a primitive drumbeat.

Jonny's inner consciousness begins vibrating like a violin string, and his essence tunes to a higher frequency. Oscillating faster and faster, he's mysteriously transported to the center of a distant galaxy, encountering an event horizon surrounding a black hole. Extreme gravitational forces stretch his molecular structure beyond recognition, and his neural circuitry melds with an advanced consciousness as he's violently sucked into a cosmic wormhole, entering a new perceptual dimension in space-time.

His newborn eyes slowly open, and he discovers that he's seated beside an immense bonfire. He's deliriously pounding on a small drum in the middle of a Native American tribal ceremony. He pauses to wipe away a stream of sweat running down his face, and is disturbed to discover that it's mixed with blood from his forehead.

Jonny is at the center of an ancient, ancestral ritual celebrating the bounty of a bison hunt. A dozen fervent sacred-fire dancers wear buffalo masks and animal hides, draped around them like furry capes.

"Tatanka, Tatanka, Tatanka!" they chant, as Jonny pounds his beaver-skin-covered drum ever faster, sweat and blood streaking his face. Across from him, several worshippers, in feathered headdresses, huddle around a severed bison head, displayed on a tall wooden alter. The worshippers burn herbal incense powder in a teak bowl beside the horned spirit-animal.

A tribal shaman, adorned with white whooping crane feathers, approaches Jonny. He hands him a wooden bowl filled with bison blood. The shaman speaks, solemnly: "Take this, new one, drink, share the life-force of our brethren, the bison. *Know these ways are true.*"

Jonny lifts the bowl to his trembling lips. Sipping in spiritual communion, he's suddenly grabbed by the shoulders and yanked up, up, up from the depth of Founder's Lake – *by Blaze Whitefeather.*

Bren cries out as she reaches over the side of the Alumacraft and grabs Jonny by his shirt collar. Together, Bren and Blaze struggle to pull Jonny back into the boat.

Blaze and Jonny lie on the bottom of the vessel, gasping for air. Bren tries her best to give mouth-to-mouth resuscitation to Jonny, who appears unconscious and is bleeding from his left temple.

Blaze, soaked and winded, crawls to the front of the boat and begins furiously paddling back to shore.

It's 4:00 AM and Lawton's Comanche County Memorial Hospital feels deserted.

Jonny, lying on his back, slowly opens his eyes and tries to focus. There's an elderly American Indian, wearing blue scrubs and hairnet, hovering over him. "Welcome back," says the care-giver, concern stamped on his weathered face.

"Who're you?" Jonny moans.

"Night nurse, checking your vitals." He places a thermometer in Jonny's mouth. "You had quite a ride last night. Didn't think you'd come back."

Jonny tries to focus. "Where am I?"

"Try to relax," the nurse replies, wrapping Jonny's arm with a blood-pressure cuff.

"How long have I been here?" The nurse places his palm on Jonny's forehead, generating a burst of static electricity. "Yeow!" Jonny winces.

"Five or six hours," the nurse replies, checking his watch. "The doctor won't be here till eight." He reads Jonny's blood pressure and removes the thermometer from his mouth. "You check out pretty good. I suggest you get some sleep."

Jonny glances around the room, still having trouble focusing. Groping around, he realizes there's an IV in his right arm and a bandage on his left temple. He tries to recall what happened hours earlier at the lake. He can't. He turns to question the nurse but he's gone.

Jonny knows he's dreaming, yet it all seems so real: He's walking across the narrow pedestrian bridge that spans Medicine Creek near the center of town. Directly in front of him, his night-nurse, still in blue scrubs and hairnet, suddenly appears.

The nurse solemnly speaks. "There's an old native legend, Jonny, about a man, standing on a whale, fishing for minnows. And you, my boy, are standing on a whale."

In the distance, Jonny hears a voice call to him. He turns, facing north toward the big lake. He spots Blaze Whitefeather, 30 yards away, perched on top of the Lawtonka dam. Blaze waves to him and holds up a large fishing net. "Hey, Jonny!" he yells. *"Guess who I just caught?"*

A short time later at the hospital, Jonny awakens to discover *another* night nurse hovering over him. This time, it's a young colored woman wearing green scrubs. Her hair is piled high on her head, teased, and sprayed into a bouffant that accentuates her pretty face.

Jonny, still groggy, mutters, "You look like Diana Ross."

"Say what?"

"You know. The Supremes."

She laughs. "Thank you but no, I'm Melinda. Don't you remember me, hon?" Jonny gives her a blank look. "Lieutenant Tate's wife. We met at the Parker party in Elgin."

It finally sinks in. "Oh. Yeah. Melinda."

"I'm here to change your bandage before the doctor arrives." She inspects the gauze affixed to his left temple. "Oh, and I'd like you to meet my brother, LaRon." Melinda moves aside to reveal 18-year-old LaRon, standing next to the bed. "I need to change *his* bandage, too."

When LaRon leans over, Jonny sees that his black face and arms are caked with dirt. LaRon says, "She dug me up to show you what *murder* looks like."

"And hate," Melinda adds. "Don't forget hate."

"Oh, yeah." LaRon replies. "Here, Jonny, look."

LaRon leans over and rips the bandage from his neck, exposing a deep bloody slit. Jonny, forcing himself to confront it, is nearly blinded by a beam of light shooting out from the wound.

"Now, look to the right," the doctor instructs Jonny, shining his pen light into Jonny's left eye. "Good." He turns to Jonny's mother, Janet, sitting on the other side of the hospital bed. "Well, he's had a pretty severe concussion. I suggest keeping him here for another day or so while we do some blood work. Most importantly, he needs bed-rest."

"Honey, you nearly drowned," Janet says, squeezing Jonny's hand. "And I'm worried about your head."

"I'm okay, Mom."

"Let's *hope* you're okay," the doctor replies. "I'll swing back later this afternoon."

Janet thanks the doctor and watches him exit. She turns her attention back to Jonny. "Bren called me last night. Around midnight. I've been in the waiting room ever since, worried sick."

"Where is she?"

"You were unconscious for hours!"

"Bren. Where is she?"

"She and Blaze were both here…until I showed up, then they went home. They said they'd be back later."

Jonny, lost in thought, finally replies, "You know, Mom, I think Blaze saved me. From drowning."

"Well, bless him for that but you shouldn't have been out there on that boat, all alone at night. It's dangerous, Jonny." They sit together in silence. Finally, Janet says, "You know, when your father had hard decisions to make, he always made a list. He put all the 'pros' in one column and the 'cons' in another."

"Yeah?"

"And I've been thinking about whether we should go back to St. Louis before the end of the year. For the new semester at Clayton. You could still graduate on time."

"Maybe."

Janet sighs. "There're several good reasons to return – in the 'pro' column. And only one in the 'con.' I thought you'd be safer in this little town. But now, I'm not so sure."

Jonny massages his temple. "Let's talk about it later, okay? Cause right now, it hurts to think."

Janet smiles. After a moment, she confides something: "I'm worried about you, Jonny. *Worried about us*."

Jonny ties to sit up, but can't. "Whaddaya mean?"

"I think there're some pretty strange things going on around here."

Jonny considers this. "Yeah. That's safe to say."

It's a cloudy, chilly morning in mid-November. Inside the Medicine Man Cafe, across the street from the Civic Center, the breakfast counter and adjacent booths are filled up. Sheriff Roy Smirk sits in a corner booth, finishing his coffee and perusing the Elgin Chronicle. He'd prefer to read the local news, but the Medicine Park Gazette is folding soon, and the pre-Christmas 55th anniversary edition will be its last hurrah.

Smirk puts down his paper and gazes absently at the historic black & white photos filling the walls. Most depict early settlements up and down Medicine Creek. Images include fishermen on the banks of Lawtonka and Lake Elmer Thomas. Some feature construction of the dam separating south Lawtonka from the inner Gondola pond and north creek. Ramshackle cobblestone and wooden houses dot both banks of the 20-yard wide, river-like creek.

The sheriff tosses two quarters onto the table and heads to the cash register. He's only been on the job six months, and he wonders how so many of the town's quirks go unnoticed by its long-time residents – including the entrance to the diner, with its seven foot wooden Indian in full headdress, painted in overly-bright colors. The totem greets customers as they come and go. A prominent plaque below the figure, reads:

"The knowledge possessed by Medicine People is privileged."
— United Indian Nation

As the sheriff exits the cafe, he practically bumps into an elderly couple on their way in. Jack and Phyllis Langston are long-time owners of the 'Highway 49 Bait & Tackle Shop' on the outskirts of town. Smirk not only knows Jack and Phyllis – he considers them bellwethers of the local economy.

"Say, you two look mighty hungry," Smirk says, dispersing his inexhaustible supply of small talk.

"Yes, sir!" Jack smiles, doffing his Caterpillar Tractor cap. "How're things, sheriff?"

"Can't complain. You?"

"Don't get us started!" Phyllis says, playfully tugging the sleeve of Smirk's jacket.

"No one's catching *anything* on Founder's," Jack replies. "Been over a week. Lots of bellyaching."

"That so?" Smirk replies, putting on his reflector shades.

"Beats anything we ever saw," Phyllis adds. "Hope it picks up soon."

"How're things on Lawtonka?" the sheriff asks, more out of politeness than concern.

"Oh, no complaints there. Lots of channel-cat and bass. Good trout on Gondola."

Smirk knows when to quit. "Well, thank God for small favors. You take care now."

The sheriff crosses the street and proceeds directly to the rear entrance of the Civic Center, hoping to avoid anyone who could be waiting in his office lobby. Safely behind his desk, he glances at his appointment book, determined to get to his patrol car and escape the needy clutches of his deputy, Josh Waggoner. No such luck.

"Morning, sheriff!" Waggoner chirps, poking his head through the door. Smirk nods and forces a smile. He decides to remove his sunglasses. His desk resembles a post-tornado trailer park.

"Morning. What's up, deputy?"

"Someone in the lobby to see you. She says it's urgent."

"And that 'someone' would be."

"Nina Whitefeather." Smirk looks puzzled. "Sampson's wife," Josh adds.

"Oh. Well, guess you better send her in."

After a moment, the deputy leads Nina into the office. She wears a traditional buckskin dress, and her braided black hair reaches the midpoint of her back. A beaded medicine bag is slug over her shoulder.

The sheriff rises to greet her, indicating the folding chair across from his desk. "Please, Mrs. Whitefeather, have a seat." He turns to Waggoner. "That'll be all, Josh." His deputy looks disappointed as he hesitantly backs through the door.

"Close it, please," Smirk calls out. As soon as his deputy shuts the door, Smirk graces Nina with a cursory, insincere smile.

"Okay. Now. What can I do for you this morning?"

"I hope I'm not disturbing you, sheriff."

"By the way, I want to say how sorry I am about your husband's disappearance. You'd think after all this time, there'd be some clue, some sign."

"Thank you. My people believe there's a bridge we must cross to reach the world beyond."

"You don't say?" Smirk gives her the once-over. He wonders what the hell she's talking about. "Please go on..."

Nina looks uncomfortable. "Well, as you may know, sheriff, the mayor forbids our tribe – *any tribe* – to fish in Lawtonka before dark, so we don't bother whites."

"Yeah. I heard something about that," Smirk replies, hoping to dissociate himself. "And?"

"My son, Blaze. He was trolling for trout last night near the dam. And he found something disturbing in his net." She reaches into her medicine bag and pulls out a bundle of woven cloth. She places it on the edge of Smirk's cluttered desk. "I believe, bringing this to you is the right thing to do."

She slowly, carefully unwraps the contents. Sheriff Smirk stares at it, his mind trying hard to process what he sees – a bloated, discolored right hand – bluish and swollen – severed at the wrist. Smirk's eyes now focus on the gold-plated championship ring on the index finger.

"Carter Singleton," he whispers, under his breath.

"If you say so. I don't know."

Smirk is alarmed. "Who else knows about this?"

"No one. Just me and Blaze. Not my daughters."

"Well, you definitely did the right thing." He searches her face. "Tell me, Nina. Why didn't Blaze come in with you?"

"He was afraid you'd arrest him."

This intrigues Smirk. "Really? Why would he think *that*?"

Nina shrugs. "Perhaps, the last 200 years?"

The sheriff walks briskly along East Lake Drive, a block north to the mayor's office, located on the top floor of the Oklahoma Press Association clubhouse. Wearing his patrol jacket and trooper hat, he trudges past the lobby bar and straight up a flight of stairs, arriving at the entrance to the mayor's expansive corner office. The door is closed. Since he and the mayor just spoke on the phone, Smirk doesn't bother to knock.

When he cautiously steps inside, he sees Mayor Ben Thomas standing behind his desk, pacing back and forth, lost in thought. He's dressed smartly in a kelly-green cardigan sweater and pale green, glen plaid slacks.

"Rushed right over," the sheriff says, slightly out of breath. He thinks to remove his hat.

"Where's it now? The hand?" the mayor replies, looking more worried than Smirk has ever seen him.

"In my office cabinet. I'll take it home tonight and put it in the fridge."

"Okay. Don't tell me anything more."

"Or should I put it in the freezer?"

"I don't wanna know."

"I've never stored a dead hand before."

"What else you got? In terms of evidence. Or motive."

"Well, like I said on the phone, I searched coach's office last week. Found a letter from his wife in his top drawer. Threatening divorce."

"Yeah, I know about that."

"And…looks like he has gambling debts. Big ones! Owes about 12 grand to a rancher in Elgin named Tate."

"Lost it all at my place. At the club. What else?"

"Well, there's the note the coach's assistant brought me. He found it shoved under Singleton's door a couple days after he went missing. Sonofabitch was just sittin' on it."

"What note?"

"From Whitefeather. Handwritten. Got it yesterday." He reaches into his jacket pocket and pulls out a folded sheet of paper.

"Read it to me."

The sheriff clears his throat, then proceeds:

"No way I'm playing football for you!
You said my father couldn't build on his dreams.
Ha! Your people killed *all* our dreams.
Prepare to have yours killed, motherfucker!"

The mayor is stunned. "Shit fire, Smirk. *This is one hot potato.*"

"No doubt."

"We've gotta get this off our plate. I've got an election in April."

"Don't look good. For nobody."

"What're your thoughts, sheriff? In terms of an investigation."

"Well, I wonder where *the rest of him is*. Singleton. I mean, if what Whitefeather says is true which I doubt, but 'innocent until proven,' you know. Anyway, maybe coach had a boating accident. Got chewed up in the propeller. *Could* happen. Maybe I should round up some volunteers. You know, to poke around shore. Drag Gondola pond. Send some divers into Lawtonka."

"Hold off on all that for now." The mayor's pacing gets more frenetic. "I'll tell you, this is one fucking hot potato."

"Yep, sure is."

"Well, for the time being, keep your lips sealed. Tight."

"Tight as a drum, sir."

"Don't make any moves till I give you marching orders."

"Yup."

"Clear?"

Smirk starts to reply, "Clear as Lake Lawtonka." But he thinks better of it and can only manage a dutiful nod as he turns and walks out the door, trooper hat in hand.

It's Friday, 11:00 AM. Inside Herman Lace's classroom, it's time for his weekly 'American History Round-Up.' Today's topic: Who's your favorite historical figure over the past 200 years? And why?

Herman stands in front of his desk, surveying the classroom. Nine students are present – good attendance so close to Thanksgiving.

"Sally Benton, you have the honor of going first."

Sally hesitates, then ventures a candidate. "Ben Franklin."

"Excellent choice!" Mr. Lace gives her an encouraging smile. "Why?"

"Well, 'cause he was smarter than everyone else. I mean, he knew a lot. He spoke French. And he discovered electricity. I think."

"It was the lightning rod, but you got close." Herman glances around for his next victim. "Let's see, Jonny Sparks. Who's your favorite? Last 200 years."

Jonny, still sporting a small bandage on his forehead, is prepared. "I vote for P.T. Barnum. Because he believed there's a sucker born every minute. Of course, that was back then. Today, I think we're *all* suckers."

"Well, Mr. Sparks you obviously have a bright future in politics." Lace surveys the room. "Dale Collins. Who's your history all-star?"

Dale's eyes dart around, unsure of his choice, but he decides to stick with it. "Mickey Mantle!"

"Mickey Mantle, huh?" Lace is amused. "Okay. And why is that?"

"Cause, he led the Yankees to the World Series last season." Dale's proud of himself. "And he makes 100,000 bucks a year. That's more than an astronaut! And he's from Oklahoma!"

"Collins, your fountain of knowledge is overwhelming but awfully leaky."

Several students laugh. Herman Lace's attention is suddenly drawn to his closed classroom door. Betty Allen is tapping on the see-through glass, signaling she wants a word. Herman cracks open the door and Betty whispers to him. Herman looks disturbed. He swings it open, allowing Sheriff Smirk and Deputy Waggoner to enter.

Smirk is all business. "Blaze Whitefeather." He glances around, spotting Blaze in the back row, slumped down in his chair. "To the front of the room, Son!" Blaze doesn't budge. He looks determined not to cooperate. Smirk signals deputy Waggoner to follow him to Blaze's chair, where they force him to his feet. The sheriff grabs handcuffs from the back of his belt and snaps them around Whitefeather's wrists.

Smirk stands back, announcing for all to hear: "Blaze Whitefeather, we're taking you to the county courthouse for questioning, in the death of Carter Singleton."

Sheriff Smirk's patrol car is parked on the driveway in front of the school entrance. As Smirk and Waggoner lead Whitefeather out the door, they're followed by what appears to be Herman Lace's entire 11:00 AM class, who curiously surround the black & white. The deputy opens the back door to accommodate their bewildered captive.

Jonny Sparks, with a bird's-eye view of the action, sees Principal Allen whisper encouragement to Blaze before Smirk shoves him into the car. The school janitor, standing next to Jonny, mutters something under his breath.

"What?" Jonny replies, turning to face Buddy Allen.

"I was saying, rumor has it, they're charging him for murder."

"You gotta be kidding!" Jonny feels his throat tighten.

The patrol car slowly pulls away, with Blaze looking helplessly at his classmates through the rear window. Buddy Allen shouts, "Whitefeather! Whatever you do, stay outta prison!"

Jonny stares incredulously at the black & white as Smirk maneuvers it onto Tackle Box Road. In an instant, Jonny bolts toward the parking lot, fumbling for his car keys. He feels completely numb, yet he's clear on one thing. He's driving straight home to tell his mother everything that just happened.

She'll know what to do.

Scattered Showers

"There are decades when nothing happens, and weeks when decades happen."

Vladimir Lenin
Moscow, Russia

Back home on Merry Circle Drive, Jonny's certain his mother knows what to do about Blaze Whitefeather's dilemma. She doesn't. At least right away. Sitting beside Jon on the tattered living room sofa, Janet gives him a reassuring pat on the shoulder.

"Where'd you say they took him?" she asks.

"The county courthouse. Where's that, anyway?"

"In Lawton, I think. We'll have to ask around."

Jonny stands up and anxiously paces. "He couldn't have done it, Mom! They handcuffed him in front of everyone, treated him like he's guilty. And I couldn't do anything about it!"

"Well, no one could. I'm sure it's all a misunderstanding."

"You should've seen the way everyone looked at him. It's not fair!"

"Probably not. But there's a lot in life that isn't." Janet tries to remain calm and measured, but Jonny can't – and he bolts out the door. Janet follows, anxiously watching from the front steps as he runs up the street, heading toward the center of town.

Jonny sits on the curb in front of Bren Lace's house. It's 2:00 PM and he's been waiting almost an hour for her to come home from school. She usually gets out early on Friday. "She'll be here soon," he keeps telling himself – although the reliability of her rusted-out, beat-up '52 Ford is a daily crapshoot. In the interim, his runaway neural circuitry replays images of Blaze Whitefeather being led out of the classroom, shoved into the police car and then driven away, staring helplessly out the window.

A horn honk shakes Jonny from his reverie. He's startled to see a burgundy and white '56 Chevy pull to the curb a few feet from him. *What the hell?* His mother emerges from the car. Jonny stands up to face her. She looks shaken.

"Mom? Are you okay?"

"I've been looking all over for you!" Janet replies in a quivering voice.

"*What is it?*"

"President Kennedy's been shot in Dallas."

Jonny's not sure he heard her correctly. "He was *what*?"

"The President. Shot in the head. He died an hour ago. It's all over the news." She motions for him to get in the car. "Come on, let's go home."

Jonny is slow to process all this. But that night, after watching hours of solemn television coverage with his mom, the tragedy slowly sinks in. His mother tries to stop crying, but can't. "He was so young!" she sobs. "And poor Jackie, so beautiful and brave, splattered with blood."

Jonny doesn't cry, but he'd like to. Most of all, he wants to share his feelings with Bren about the day's disturbing events. Surely, her father told her about Blaze. After all, it was *his* classroom. But what else does she know? And how does she feel about the assassination? He decides to call her, but her father's the one who answers the phone.

"Sorry, Jon boy. She's out. Probably be back late. Late o'clock. I'll tell her you called. Take care, Son. Bye."

Mr. Lace sounded weird, Jonny thought after hanging up. And he slurred some of his words. Was he drinking? And where was Bren on Friday night at 10 o'clock?

Jonny told his mother goodnight, gave her a hug, and went to bed. He had a lot on his mind, so much to process – and yet, he was exhausted. He needed to sleep. Or at least try. One thing he knew for sure. This was one of the worst days of his life.

After the horror of seeing the bodies of his father and grandparents lifted into the back of an ambulance last summer in St. Louis – how could he have known:

Grief, like lightning, can strike randomly and often. And when it does, it defies measurement or comparison. It's simply grief.

Jonny couldn't have been asleep more than an hour before he was awakened by a tap-tap-tapping on the window next to his nightstand. Groggy, he peers out the side of the shade to get a furtive look at who or what could possibly be making that noise. And at this hour.

It's Bren! She waves to him, mouthing, "Jonny!" – a blast of vapor streaming out of her mouth into the cold night air. She's wrapped in a heavy down parka, hugging her shoulders, trying to keep warm.

Jonny raises the shade and slides open the window. "What're you doing here?" he whispers through the screen, trying not to wake his mom.

"I gotta get home but maybe we can meet up tomorrow? For lunch, maybe?"

"What's tomorrow, Saturday?" Jonny's still trying to wake up.

"Yeah. Meet me on the sidewalk by the creek. Near the bridge. At noon?"

"Okay. By the bridge, right?"

"I'll bring lunch – we gotta catch up – see ya tomorrow!"

And just like that, she was gone.

Jonny, sleeping later than usual – even for a Saturday morning – hastily departs his house, walking two blocks west, reaching the bank of Medicine Creek at straight-up noon.

The sun is out but there's a late-November chill in the air. Wearing faded jeans, a sweater and wool car coat, Jonny walks the sidewalk north for a quarter mile, arriving at the base of the pedestrian bridge that spans the width of the creek. The narrow 120-foot wooden structure is painted all-white, with high latticed side railings. It evokes memories of Jonny's strange encounter with his hospital care-giver the night he nearly drowned on Founder's Lake. "It was just a dream," he reminds himself.

Jonny glances at his watch: Ten past noon. Where the hell is Bren? Finally, he spots her walking toward him in the distance. She seems unreasonably cheerful, considering the recent tumultuous events. He's pleasantly surprised by her disposition, and especially likes what she's wearing: a red fog coat with plaid scarf, skin-tight black pedal pushers and cowboy boots. She totes a patchwork blanket in one hand and a brown paper sack in another.

"Hi!" she chirps, holding up the bag. "I made us lunch. Ham and cheese sandwiches. With carrot sticks and Hostess cupcakes." She grabs Jonny's hand and squeezes it as she surveys the area near the pond. "Your hands are cold!"

"Lots of people out today," Jonny replies. "Tourists, I think."

"Yeah. I don't know why they fish in this weather. That's what Alaska's for."

"Let's take a walk," Jonny says, indicating the near-empty creek bank on the other side of the bridge. "There's a table over there."

Bren smiles and nods in agreement. They walk in silence toward the bridge. After a moment, Jonny blurts out, "I called you last night."

"Yeah. Dad told me this morning."

"Where were you?" There's a hint of accusation in his voice.

"Me? Visiting friends."

After an uncomfortable pause, Jonny replies, "Parker Tate?"

"No, no. Old friends. Family friends."

"Family?"

"Yeah. Sort of." After another uncomfortable silence, Bren pivots. "I'm sure Blaze didn't have anything to do with Coach Singleton. They're just trying to find someone to pin it on."

They stop in the middle of the bridge and gaze north toward the Lawtonka dam and the vast lake beyond. Jonny, avoiding Bren's eyes, says, "You know, I hate it here. Most days I can't wait to go back." Jonny pauses, then decides to push on. "To tell you the truth, you're the only thing I like about this place. I like you a lot, Bren. But you're making it hard for me."

"Whaddaya mean?"

"Remember the fight we had in my car, after you introduced me to Parker Tate? At Blaze's place?"

"Sure. I told you I wanted to *do something* with my life. With music. And I asked if you felt the same…maybe we could do it together."

"Yeah, well…sometimes I don't trust you."

Bren turns to face him. "Why not? Parker?"

He still avoids looking at her. "I'm just telling you how I feel."

More silence. Then, Bren takes a leap. "Okay. Jonny, look at me." Jonny slowly turns to face her. "You have Dale Collins in one of your classes, right?"

"Yeah, your dad's history class. And English Lit. He's a jerk."

"I'm sure he seems that way. But I had a big crush on him. We dated last year. For a short time."

"You're kidding me."

"I know it seems weird. But we did."

"Jesus."

"I'm trusting you with this, Jonny."

"Okay. Go on."

"He got me pregnant."

Jonny's stunned. All he can do is wince.

"I carried the baby all last year at school. I hid it until spring. Then I had to drop out. People were saying ugly things."

"Yeah, I'm sure…"

"I had the baby. A boy. And I gave him up to Dale's older brother and his wife. For adoption. They live in Kansas."

"I don't know what to say."

"That's where I was last night. They came down with the baby and I went to see him. Probably for the last time." Bren bites her lip. "It really hurt." Jonny sighs. "I couldn't stop crying last night when I got home."

"I'm sorry," Jonny whispers, searching her face.

"Well, I finally realized I'm not. Sorry, I mean. I know I did the right thing. For everybody. They couldn't have kids, and anyway. Here I am." She forces a smile.

Jonny feels strangely relieved. "So that's what you meant by 'family get-together.'"

"I don't see Dale anymore. I wish him well and everything. But at a distance."

Jonny finally exhales. "Well, thanks for telling me. It must've been hard."

"You're one of the few who knows."

Jonny takes her hand. "Bren, no matter what, I'm glad I met you."

"Me too." She smiles and takes Jonny's other hand. "Hey, if nothing else, maybe we can make some music together."

Later that afternoon, Janet enters the Gazette newspaper office in the center of town, one block east of the creek. She immediately senses the paper's days are numbered. Boxes are stacked in the corner near the front window. In the opposite corner, a green Royal manual typewriter lies on an empty metal desk. In the center of the room, Janet recognizes the clunky Heidelberg hot-type printing press – a small version of the linotype machines used by the St. Louis Post-Dispatch, before moving to offset photocomposition.

"Perfect," Janet says out loud, amused by the crude process responsible for the Gazette's weekly assemblage of local news and mom & pop advertising.

"*Far from perfect*," says an attractive, silver-haired man emerging from an adjacent storage room. He carries a stack of newspapers to a nearby cabinet and plops them down. "But it's good enough for our final printing." He scrutinizes Janet and likes what he sees. "Name's Chandler. Call me Vic. Can I help you?"

"The door was open," Janet says, trying to sound apologetic but isn't. She's in too much of a hurry for small talk.

"Nothing here to steal." He turns to indicate the Heidelberg. "Interested in an outdated printer? I'm practically giving it away."

Janet smiles, shakes her head. "Betty Allen said maybe you'd help…" Vic gives her a quizzical look. "…with a single-page flier. Around three dozen copies. By early next week."

"Betty, huh. Lovely woman." Vic rubs his chin, thinks. "What's this about?"

"An announcement. We're holding a candlelight service Wednesday night. At the pier on Founder's Lake."

"You don't say."

"To honor President Kennedy."

"Oh. That's nice." Vic gives her another close look. "Tell you what. I'm doing a proof run of our final edition Monday. I could do it later in the afternoon. All I'll need from you – is *copy*. How's that sound?"

Janet flashes a big smile. "Perfect."

The sun is setting on Founder's Lake. Betty Allen distributes small white candles to over 30 townsfolk who congregate in the small parking lot beside the pier. The wind has inexplicably died down, providing a window of eerie calm.

"This was a good idea," Janet whispers to Betty. For days, citizens of Medicine Park huddled around their black & white TV sets, watching coverage of the President's funeral procession as the casket moved from the White House to the U.S. Capitol, then on to Arlington National Cemetery. These solemn images were interspersed with replays of the surrealistic assassination of *JFK's assassin*. So, after the morning-till-night broadcast of one of America's greatest tragedies, well, townsfolk savored an opportunity to gather and commiserate, face-to-face.

As nightfall approaches, Betty and Janet work together to help participants light their candles. Herman Lace is first to carry his wax torch onto the pier. His face beams as he watches his daughter, Bren – along with Jonny Sparks and Parker Tate – standing at the far end of the runway, strumming acoustic guitars and singing Bob Dylan's new protest anthem, "Blowin' in the Wind."

One by one, the participants follow Herman onto the pier, huddling around the crooning trio, whose voices blend in a tribute to social injustice and lost causes.

Then, suddenly, the minstrels stop playing as they notice onlookers pointing out toward the reservoir and gasping in disbelief. The singers turn to see thousands of bloated fish bobbing on the surface of the water. Within minutes, the flotilla of dead channel catfish and largemouth bass numbers in the *hundreds of thousands*.

Those witnessing this inexplicable event are aghast. Speechless. Many begin crying. And in this stunning, candle-lit moment, their tears are no longer reserved for a dead president.

The following morning, when Janet Sparks enters the Gazette newspaper office she discovers owner Vic Chandler hard at work, fitting a lead-filled cardboard matt around the press cylinder of his outdated printer. He doesn't bother to look up. "Morning. Be right with ya."

Janet inspects the green Royal manual on the desk near the front window. "How much for the typewriter?" she asks.

"Not for sale."

"Really?"

Vic finally stops tinkering and looks up to acknowledge her. "Take it, it's yours. Christmas came early."

Janet's pleasantly surprised. "Why, thank you, Santa!" She looks him up and down. "What's with you, anyway?"

"Whaddaya mean?"

"You wouldn't even charge me for printing the flyers."

Vic inspects his soiled hands and wipes them on a nearby rag. "By the way," he says, "your candlelight service. Last night. How was it?"

Janet rolls her eyes. "Well. Let's just say we had uninvited guests."

"You mean the dead fish?"

"You heard about that?"

"Lady, I'm the Medicine Park Gazette. I know everything around here." He glances at the old Royal. "What're gonna do with the typewriter?"

"Oh. I may write a story. Might send it to an old colleague in St. Louis at the Post-Dispatch."

"Good paper. What's the idea?"

"It's, uh about the strange things happening around here. He's one of those 'True Crime' writers. Been his beat for years. Who knows, he might do something with it."

"Got a title yet?"

"A couple possibilities. One is Big Mysteries in a Small Town."

"Hmm. Could work. Next?"

"How about Life Gets Dark in Medicine Park."

"Whoa! Bingo. *Now* you've got my juices flowing!"

"You like it?"

"Got a real winner there, kiddo. I say we celebrate your return to journalism."

Janet and Vic sit at a booth inside the **Medicine Man Cafe**. Vic starts to eat his last bite of pecan pie, thinks better of it and lays down his fork.

Vic eyes Janet's empty plate. "Sure you don't want another slice?"

"No, thanks. One is enough. But when you see our waitress, I'll take more coffee."

"Done." He looks around, but can't flag anyone. "Pretty busy today!"

Janet's gazes at him. "You lived here all your life, Vic? I don't remember seeing you when I was growing up."

"Oh, heavens, no. Ten, eleven years maybe. I had a good business in Oklahoma City. When my wife died, back in '52, I decided to sell it. Took early retirement and moved here to help my son with the newspaper. He was having a hard time making a go of it."

"Not much of a retirement."

Vic grins. "*You can say that again.*"

"Your son lives here?"

He nods. "Korean war vet. You can imagine, it's an easy glide from Fort Sill to Medicine Park. Folks do it all the time."

"What's he doing, now that you're shutting down the paper?"

"Well, thankfully, he landed a job with the Chronicle. In Elgin." The waitress finally arrives at their table and refills their cups. Vic gives her an appreciative wink.

"You're a surprising man," Janet says, catching Vic off guard.

"You think?" he replies, trying to sound nonchalant. She smiles, nods. Vic considers this. "You know, Betty Allen told me a bit about you. Not much, but enough to give me the feeling we have a lot in common."

She's intrigued. "Do we, now?"

"For the time being, though, I'd like to focus on our mutual interests – in the here and now."

"Meaning?"

"Your story about all the strange things happening around here. I'd like to help you with that. And I'm thinking maybe the best place to start is by putting pressure on the right guy."

The Oklahoma Press Association clubhouse, dedicated in 1911 by Medicine Park founder JWE Thomas, was a decades-long hangout for roving newspapermen, backbench politicians, and scoundrels of all stripes. The long, two-story cobblestone and concrete exterior featured a recessed outdoor porch with eight vertical pillars to support the top floor overhang. The porch was a popular place to congregate – with its unobstructed view of Medicine Creek, just beyond the town's main road.

Inside, the club's elongated first floor featured a lobby bar that functioned as a cheerful gateway to the maze of dining booths and pool tables beyond. At the end of the hall, three coin-operated telephone booths were constantly occupied.

Today, the first floor – beyond the bar – resembles an empty warehouse, with only a corner shoeshine stand remaining from its glory days. The rear kitchen, long closed, was significantly damaged by the previous summer's tornado. Former upstairs press offices are now reserved for Mayor Ben Thomas.

On this rainy morning in late November, the mayor enters the clubhouse and, as usual, heads straight to the lobby bar for a tall Irish coffee. Sipping his brew and chatting with the barkeep, he notices a few patrons gathered around the bulletin board near the stairs leading up to his office. They're pointing to a faux newspaper spread pinned onto the board.

The onlookers make way for the mayor, who leans in to get a closer look at the large headline that reads:

Life Gets Dark in Medicine Park!

The mayor can't believe his eyes as he scans the bold subheads underneath:

– War Hero Mysteriously Vanishes
– Football Coach Brutally Murdered
– A Million Lake Fish Dead

In the bottom corner of the provocative story, Janet Spark's name and phone number appear.

The mayor's face transforms from pale to red. He yanks the spread from the bulletin board and bounds up the stairs to his office.

Janet sits at her dining room table, tentatively fingering the keys on her recently acquired typewriter. She's interrupted by loud banging on her front door, accompanied by an insistent doorbell. She slides her Royal manual to the corner of the table and moves her gleaming coffee percolator center stage.

She opens her front door, fully expecting to see the mayor. He holds the mock newspaper spread up to her face. "What the hell's *this* about?"

"Come in out of the rain, mayor!" She motions him inside. "Like some coffee?"

"*I'd prefer an explanation*!" he replies, brushing past her on his way into the living room.

Janet attempts small talk as the mayor reluctantly joins her at the table. He silently fumes as she pours fresh brew into her mother's favorite chinaware. The mayor can no longer contain himself. "Okay, sweetheart, let's get to it. I'm a busy man."

"I know you are!" Janet replies, savoring the exchange. "Look, Your Honor, there's an election in April. You think you can sweep this craziness under the rug, and just wait it out? Whistle past the graveyard?"

"Oh. I see," he says, sarcastically. "You're dispensing political advice."

"All I'm saying, mayor, if you wanna be reelected, you better get out in front of all this. Start owning this thing. People around here are nervous. Scared, even."

Ben Thomas is running low on patience. "Jesus! Get to the point, hon."

"Okay. First point: Don't call me 'hon.' My name is Janet."

It's Wednesday, December 3, 6:30 PM. Inside the Press Association clubhouse, Mayor Ben Thomas and Sheriff Roy Smirk sit behind a folding table at the far end of the cavernous first-floor echo chamber. Sixty folding chairs, filled with townsfolk, are arranged in rows facing the front table. Additional attendees stand in the back near the lobby bar.

The mayor gavels the gathering to order and speaks into his microphone. "Okay, everyone! Can I have your attention? Please?" The crowd noise descends from a roar to a collective murmur. "Thank you. Welcome to our, I guess you'd call it a Town Hall."

"And it's about time!" shouts an old-timer from the back.

The mayor ignores him. "Sheriff Smirk and I are here to give you an update on some issues. Stuff I know you've been concerned about."

The mayor pauses to assess his audience. "Now, I guess you could also call this a press conference. Reporters are here from the Elgin Chronicle and the Lawton Constitution. So, a special welcome to 'em." He spots one of the writers near the front and gives him a wink and a smile. "Okay, first, I'll turn this thing over to Sheriff Smirk for an update on the Carter Singleton murder case. Sheriff?"

Roy Smirk, uniform pressed and badge shined, pulls his microphone closer and clears his throat. "Good evening, folks. I wish this get-together wasn't necessary. But I suppose it is. So." He knows he's onstage and the pressure's on. "The coach's hand was violently severed at the wrist, and that's about all we know for sure. The primary suspect is Blaze Whitefeather. The county has assigned him a defense attorney. Whitefeather claims he fished the hand out of Lawtonka near the dam."

A voice interrupts from the back. "How ya know it's the coach's hand?"

The mayor jumps in. "Please…hold your questions till the sheriff's finished."

Smirk continues. "We know it's his hand, because there's a 1953 Division 3 championship ring on the right finger. Custom inlays with gold crystal. Same one coach wore every day for years. But to your point, when Whitefeather's mom brought it in to me, the hand was bloated waterlogged. So, there's no way to pull prints. Okay? Also, I think you should know that Whitefeather pleaded 'not guilty' at his preliminary hearing last Tuesday. But the judge has denied him bail." He pauses. "Oh – trial's set for the first of the year. Okay, I'll open it to questions."

In the middle of the crowd, Janet Sparks stands and confronts Smirk. "You don't have a body, sheriff. No witnesses. No evidence, really. And you say no bail? To me, that smacks of racism."

"Racism?" the sheriff retorts. "We treat folks equal in this county! Whites, blacks, browns, reds. And I'd like to point out, this ain't our jurisdiction, anyway. This belongs to the county. It's no longer a Medicine Park issue."

The mayor leans into his microphone. "To your point, Janet, there's definitely circumstantial evidence, and it'll all come out at the trial. We just need to keep a cool head and let the justice system play out."

A woman shouts from the back. "And who's on trial for the murder of a million fish?"

The mayor takes the lead. "Okay, settle down. Next week, the state Department of Wildlife folks are running a test on the water. To determine the source of the kill."

"*Next week?*" shouts an incredulous man from the audience.

The mayor talks over him. "They'll also do an autopsy on the fish. Our wildlife team's moving as fast as they can. They're netting 'em up as soon as they die off. At this point, it's a total mystery." The mayor recognizes a waving hand in the crowd. "I see Herman Lace has a question. Herman?"

"Just an observation, Mr. Mayor. Or, better yet, a theory."

"All ears, Herman. Shoot."

Herman stands to address the group. "Most of you know my son works in munitions at Fort Sill. And with this whole run-up to Vietnam, they're bringing in cases and cases of artillery shells. For tanks and mortars and howitzers and such."

"Will this turn into a seminar?" the sheriff interjects, sarcastically.

"Not unless you'd like one!" Herman bandies back. Some participants laugh.

The mayor tries to keep it on track. "Go on, Lace. But make it quick."

"Thank you! Okay, so, the base has just opened a spray plant to coat the shells with zinc chromate. Which protects 'em from corrosion. And they pour the waste in drums and haul 'em to a chemical dump, about 20 miles past the wildlife refuge."

The mayor's running out of patience. "Does this story have an ending, Herman?"

"A *sad ending,* I think. 'Cause Clyde Trainer tells me he sees military convoys pull off Highway 49, near Little Medicine Creek. Maybe they're dumping the stuff. Which is poisonous. Carcinogenic. Soldiers are pouring cancer into the creek that feeds into Founder's."

The room fills with a vocal undercurrent of outrage and disgust.

From the back, a scraggly man in overalls – a stranger to most – rises to his feet and yells, "Don't ya think there's a connection between the dead fish, and the aliens they spotted last week near Roswell?"

After another burst of buzz-saw murmuring, the mayor reestablishes control of the crowd.

"I gotta say, folks, we've heard more conspiracy theories tonight than those investigating the Kennedy assassination."

It's time for an American History lesson at Medicine Park High. Herman Lace stands with his back to the class, writing the United States presidential line of succession on the blackboard:

Vice President

Speaker, House of Representatives

President pro tempore, Senate

He underlines the words 'Vice President' with white chalk. He turns to face the class. "Now, friends and neighbors since Lyndon Baines Johnson was sworn in as our 36th president, this order of succession is a moot point. But our founding fathers carefully considered how we should address potential calamities, where entire layers of government could be wiped out." He pauses to survey the class. "Are you getting any of this, Mr. Collins?"

Dale Collins, wearing his omnipresent letter jacket, snaps to attention. "Uh, yes sir. At least I think so, sir."

"Could you give us an example of such a calamity?"

Dale looks stymied. "Uh, I dunno. Maybe an atomic bomb?"

Jonny Sparks, seated across the room, glares at him with contempt. Mr. Lace, however, is encouraged. "Not bad, Dale. You certainly know your calamities." Several classmates laugh. "Mr. Sparks, you've been writing something all morning. Is it a secret, or can you share it with us?"

Jonny hesitates, then blurts, "It's a poem, Mr. Lace. For your daughter."

After school, Jonny awaits Bren's return from Elgin High, sitting – as usual – on the curb in front of her house. He hopes she beats her father home. Today, thankfully she does. Jonny watches eagerly as she emerges from her battered '52 Ford, with several books nestled in her arm.

Minutes later, they sit together on the screened-in front porch, accompanied by an electric floor heater. Bren rolls cigarettes from her pouch. "I talked to Parker today."

"Oh?" Jonny's still uncertain about her relationship with him.

"He thinks we should pull our guitars and amps out of Blaze's shed and move 'em back to his place. His house has lots of space."

"Too much space, don't ya think? I mean, it's a cave. Bad acoustics."

"He says there's a good room upstairs. And we're not recording anything. Yet."

"We need to start playing in front of people." Jonny takes a smoke from her and lights it up.

"Yeah, I've been thinking about that." They sit in silence for a few moments, blowing rings.

"I wrote you something today," Jonny says, hesitantly.

"You did? What?"

"A poem. It's only a few lines."

"Can I see it?" Jonny reluctantly pulls a folded index card from his back pocket and holds it out to her. "I changed my mind," she tells him. "I want you to read it to me."

Jonny takes a deep breath. "It's about you and your baby."

"Oh," Bren says, taken aback. She braces herself. "Okay. I'm as ready as I'll ever be. I guess."

Jonny begins reading, trying not to let nerves trip him up.

"Between those who take and those who give,
There are those who choose both ways to live.
No need to doubt your choices past,
You gave the gift that's sure to last a lifetime."

Bren is stunned, but she forces a smile. "That's nice," she says, flatly. "Hey, would you like a Coke? I'm getting one for myself."

"Sure," Jonny replies, watching her jump up and head to the kitchen. He feels like he's going to throw up. He sits, paralyzed, wishing he could drive away in his car before she comes back.

When Bren returns to the porch, Coke bottles in hand, she places them on the floor beside her chair. She slides onto Jonny lap and throws her arms around him. Her eyes are red and puffy. "Thanks for my poem," she whispers. "I love it. It made me cry." She kisses him on the cheek, then plants one firmly on his lips. It's a long, sincere, moist kiss and Jonny wishes he could freeze the moment forever.

That night, Jonny has trouble falling asleep. His mind keeps replaying the feeling of Bren's lips on his, and the way she gently brushed her fingers across his neck.

He finally drops off to a disturbed dreamland, where he inexplicably finds himself struggling underwater. His limbs are heavy and he can't propel himself in any direction. He feels like a prisoner of the deep, suddenly snagged in a large fishing net. He fights to break free. He tries to scream as he's quickly pulled to the surface.

"Come back," an observer whispers. "Breathe deep."

Jonny's eyes fly open. His vision blurred, he senses a reassuring presence standing over him. "Where's my mom?" Jonny murmurs, trying to sit up. He now realizes the elderly man by his bedside is the same native tribesman who attended to him in his hospital room in Lawton. In addition to his blue nursing scrubs, he wears a white-feathered headdress, like the shaman who offered him bison blood during his earlier, peyote-induced time-travel to a distant world.

The care-giver leans closer to Jonny. "Remember the big oak near the picnic table? Beside the creek?"

Jonny, his throat hoarse, struggles to talk. "You mean where me and Bren had lunch that day?"

The tribesman nods. "There is great insight from that tree. Go to it. Put your arms around it. Feel its bark. Seek guidance."

"I don't know what you mean."

The shaman holds a wooden bowl to Jonny's lips. "Drink of the tree spirit. Discover there is no single branch to the truth."

Jonny takes the thick liquid in his mouth and immediately spits it out. "Fuck! *What is that?* It's rotten."

"Not rotten. Tree sap."

Jonny tosses the bowl across the room, yelling, "Please, someone let me out!"

"Jonny, wake up!" his mother repeats, gently shaking him. Jonny looks startled, trying to comprehend his dead-of-night situation. She presses her palm to his forehead. "You were screaming, hon. Were you having a bad dream?"

"Yeah must've…" Jonny looks around, groggy. "What time is it?"

"It's the middle of the night. Can you go back to sleep?"

Jonny now recognizes his mother's silhouette, barely visible in his dark bedroom. "I need to go to the creek tomorrow," he tells her. "Early. Can I cut school?"

"Oh, I don't know, Jon," she replies, thinking better of it.

"And will you come with me?"

Early the following morning, Jonny and Janet Sparks stand beside the picnic table on the west bank of the creek, a short distance from the pedestrian bridge. Jonny scrutinizes the scraggly oak tree nearby. A large leafless branch juts out over the water. It's perfect for climbing, and he wonders how many kids have frightened themselves and their parents by crawling out too far. His ears fill with the sound of children playing nearby.

"What're you looking for, exactly?" Janet asks, placing her brown wicker basket on the bench.

"Well, in my dream, the nurse, the medicine man said if I got up close to the tree, put my arms around it, I'd see something I need to see. Or feel something. I know it sounds weird."

"Yes, it does."

"But I keep having dreams like that. Maybe I should pay attention."

"Okay. So, whaddaya want me to do with the camera?" She rummages inside her basket and pulls out a 35 mm Canon AE-1.

"Why'd that guy give you that?"

"That *guy* is publisher of the Gazette. Vic Chandler. He loaned it to me. Although he has a habit of giving me things," she mutters to herself.

"Did you get some good pictures?" Jonny asks. "At Founder's?"

"I think so, yeah. There's a back road leading up to the dam and I walked out to the middle and got some overhead shots. The wildlife guys are still netting the dead fish. Frogs and turtles, too. It's a mess!"

"Any idea what happened?"

"Won't know for a week or so." Janet pulls a thermos from the basket. "Like some coffee?"

"Yeah sure. I never drank it till we got here. Now I'm kinda hooked."

They sit across from each other on the bench. Children play nearby with their parents looking on. Trout season on the man-made Gondola pond, an off-shoot of the creek, attracts lots of tourists, even in winter.

After a moment, Jonny confides something to Janet. "You know, when we first got here, I thought we'd be long-gone by now." She flashes a knowing smile. "And, Mom, part of me wants to pack up and fly home – *tomorrow* if we could."

"I think about that every day," Janet says, filling two Styrofoam cups with coffee.

"So, what's keeping us here?"

Janet gives Jonny a searching look. "What do *you* think? Why do *you* think we're still here?"

"I dunno." He mulls it over as he sips. Janet waits patiently for him to sort it out. Jonny shakes his head. "This place is the *sticks*, Mom. *You know that.*"

She nods. "A painfully small pond. Yes."

"I miss my friends in St. Louis. I miss the city."

"Me too. I miss our house. *Even our neighbors.*"

"But, you know, in a strange way, I feel I don't know. I feel important here."

"You do?"

"Maybe I should say, I feel something important's going on. And it's pretty cool being in the middle of it."

Janet considers this. "Yeah. It's like a creepy bedtime story."

"So," Jonny replies, playfully, "we're staying here a while longer, right?"
She smiles. "At least a few more days."

Jonny chuckles. "Okay. Good. Next week, let's take another vote."

They sit quietly, sipping their coffee. After a few moments, Jonny stands up and walks to the oak tree. He looks it up and down, pondering his next move. He starts to put his arms around it, then looks over to his mom. "Will you pretend you're taking pictures? So, you know, I don't feel so silly."

Janet gets up from the bench, camera in hand, and circles around Jonny, looking though the viewfinder as he places his ear against the trunk and rubs the bark. After a moment, he looks to his mom and throws his hands up in the air. "This is stupid! I don't feel *anything*."

"Okay," Janet replies, her camera dangling from the strap around her neck. "Let's pack up."

Jonny peers through the U-shaped crotch of the tree, looking north toward the pedestrian bridge. Near the middle, he notices something hanging from the underside. He squints. "Mom," he says, pointing. "You see that? It looks like, I dunno, maybe someone's leg. A naked leg."

Janet walks toward the creek bank to get a closer look. "It *does* look like a leg! Hanging by the ankle."

"Is that blood dripping down?" Jonny replies, joining Janet at the creek bank.

Janet points to the rear of the civic building across the creek. "Jonny, run get the sheriff while I snap some pictures!" Jonny takes off as Janet wades into the cold creek, waist deep, to get a better angle on the hairy, blood-stained leg – severed at the top of the thigh – suspended beneath the bridge.

One of the little boys playing near the creek bank stops and looks out where Janet is snapping pictures. He screams at the gruesome appendage. Janet reacts to his cry. "*I bet that's Coach Singleton's leg,*" she whispers to herself. "*What kind of monster did this?*"

The following afternoon, Jonny, Bren and Parker gather inside the maintenance shed-turned-music studio on the Whitefeather family acreage. Parker, on electric guitar and Bren, on keyboards, play an intro to Roy

Orbison's plaintive ballad *Only the Lonely.* Jonny, an electric bass slung across his shoulder, begins to sing:

> Only the lonely....know the way I feel tonight
> Only the lonely know the feeling ain't right
> There goes my baby.

Parker and Bren join in: (Bop-Bop-Bop-Bop!)

> There goes my heart.
> They're gone forever

> (Bop-Bop-Bop-Bop!)

> So far apart.
> But only the lonely
> Know why – I cry
> Only the lonely!

The trio plays an instrumental outro to bring the song to a close. They look back and forth at each other, wondering what each thinks of their maiden plunge into band-world.

Parker breaks the ice. "Well, Jon, you're no Roy Orbison but you sound pretty damn good!"

Bren jumps in. "Real nice, Jonny, we all did great!"

"We should work up one of Bren's songs next," Parker adds.

There's a knock at the door. It slowly swings open to reveal Nina Whitefeather, holding an impressive-looking layer cake. She enters, smiling shyly. "Sorry to interrupt. Before our special guest arrives, I wanted to bring this 'Dream Catcher' cake. For his birthday."

"Dream Catcher?" Bren asks, clearing song sheets off a small table in the corner of the room to make way for Nina's treat.

"Yes, come look." Nina gingerly places the cake on the table for all to see. Three stacked layers are covered with white icing. On top is a circular, handmade willow hoop with three tiny white feathers dangling from it.

"Very cool!" Bren says, trying to keep from touching it.

A familiar voice calls out from the open doorway, "Hey, get away from that!" Everyone turns to see Blaze Whitefeather enter with his arms outstretched.

"Happy Birthday!" Nina says, clapping her hands. The others join in.

"Thanks, everyone!" Blaze says, throwing his arms around Parker, who gives him a delighted hug and backslap.

"Happy Birthday, Blaze!" shouts Bren, lining up to congratulate him.

"It's more like Happy Freedom Day," Blaze says, receiving hugs from both Bren and Jonny.

"We got our drummer back!" Parker yells.

"Well, for the time being, at least." Blazes replies. "They know they can't hold me any longer but I'm still under suspicion."

Jonny gives him a playful shove. "Sounds like you're on thin ice, man..."

Everyone stops to consider what Jonny just said. Jonny's eyes light up. "*Thin Ice*! You know, that should be the name of our band!"

Bren looks to Parker. "I love it!"

Parker mulls it over. "*It sounds really different.*"

Blaze jumps in. "Has a ring to it, for sure. I think we should go with it."

Parker's sold. "Okay, then. *Thin Ice* it is!"

A few days later, Betty Allen and Vic Chandler huddle with the mayor inside his second-floor office at the Press Association clubhouse. The final proofs of the six-page 55th Anniversary Edition of the Gazette are spread across the long conference table.

Ben Thomas is beaming. "You've both done a fantastic job. Photos, copy, everything looks great. I think we're ready to go!"

"*Finally,*" Vic replies, relieved.

The mayor laughs, his six-foot-four frame shaking. To him, this special supplement, distributed right before Christmas, is a bundle of joy after weeks of anxiety and distress.

"Congratulations, Ben," Betty says. "I'll let Herman Lace know he's officially off the hook."

"He did a fine job – once he dropped the *attitude.*"

There's a knock on the mayor's office door and Janet Sparks sticks her head inside. "Is everyone decent?" she says, smiling.

"By all means, come in!" the mayor replies. "Please, Janet, sit down." The mayor turns to Betty and Vic. "Can you two stay for a bit? I consider you part of my Brain Trust."

Vic laughs. "Don't think *I'd* trust us. But sure."

The mayor sits at the head of the conference table and the others gather around. After a moment, Sheriff Smirk enters, remembering to take off his trooper hat as he steps inside. "Sorry for being late," he says, surveying the room. "Wrote up lots of tickets today. Mostly parking, but the money's always welcome this close to Christmas."

"Take a load off, sheriff," the mayor says. He has a smile for everyone. "Well...I have *more* Christmas cheer: the county DA says he's retaining the prosecutor in the Singleton murder case. But the bad news is: the onus is on *us* to quickly round up a new suspect."

Smirk's mouth drops open. "I don't have the manpower for that!"

"I hear you," the mayor replies. "Where're we at with suspects? Is the coach's wife still on the radar?"

The sheriff removes his reflective shades and slides them into his top pocket. "Still got my eye on her." Smirk looks warily around the table. "Can I discuss this, Ben? You know, in front of everyone?"

"Keep going," the mayor replies.

"Okay. Well. Seems she has a new boyfriend down in Cache. Spends a lot of time at his place. Name's Higgins. He gives tours of Chief Quanah Parker's old Star House."

"Is that significant?" the mayor asks.

"No. Just a strange way to make a livin'. Anyway, this Higgins guy has a prior. He assaulted a tourist at the chief's home last year. Did 90 days. Other than that, he looks to be a garden variety low life."

Betty Allen frowns. "Rita Singleton hasn't been to church since Carter was murdered. I saw her at Langston's market, though. She was dressed inappropriately, as always. And she dropped cigarette ashes all over the produce section."

"See, that worries me," the mayor says. "We're looking for a needle in a haystack. Our killer could be a drifter, long gone by now. Or...he could live in another district. Outside our jurisdiction."

"He could be a *she*," Janet adds.

"Bingo!" Vic says. "Mayor, I think you need to cast a wider net."

"What does *that* mean?" Ben replies.

"Indulge me for a second. What's the latest on Founder's Lake?"

"You mean, the Wildlife Department investigation?" the mayor replies. Vic nods. "Well, they think a chemical killed the fish. They're trying to pin down the exact nature of it. They found the highest concentration about 50 yards from the pier."

"Next step?" Vic replies.

"Well, this Thursday, the wildlife guys are taking a barge out. They're using divers to hunt for a source. If they find anything, they'll try 'n' winch it up."

"Okay, so here's my thinking," Vic replies. "The district attorney reports to the county commissioners, right? And there's three of 'em?"

Betty nods. "Right. Representing our three districts."

"Okay. So, the DA thinks the Singleton murder case is on *us*. It's a District 3 problem. But Founder's Lake is an *all-district* issue. Folks from Elgin and Lawton fish there, right?"

"And soldiers from Fort Sill," the sheriff adds.

"Good," Vic continues. "As soon as you find more on the lake, schedule a press conference at the county courthouse. Make sure you've got TV coverage, in addition to the print guys."

Betty jumps in. "Like the Sampson Whitefeather memorial you did last August, Ben. In the lobby. That went over well."

"But bigger," Vic adds. "Do it upstairs in their Board Room."

The mayor chews on this. "To be honest, I'm not sure I follow. Janet, you've been awfully quiet. What's your take on all this?"

Janet glances around the table before she dives in. "I think what Vic's driving at, you give an update on Founder's lake and provide next steps. Then you field questions. One of us is there, asking about the Carter Singleton murder case. And you look directly to the TV cameras, and you ask viewers for help. You plead with anyone who might've seen or heard anything suspicious, to call our hot line and report it."

Sheriff Smirk looks confused. "What good will *that* do?"

"Don't you see?" Janet replies. "*We're deputizing the entire county*! The DA might not see it as a county-wide hot button, but TV viewers do. That murder scares 'em as much as it does us."

"What hot line?" Betty replies.

After a pause, Janet takes the plunge. "You can give 'em *my* number. At home. I'll track all the leads and coordinate with Sheriff Smirk. It's our best shot at this point, don't you think?"

"I like it!" the mayor says, getting to his feet. "Janet, you're officially on the payroll. I trust you accept cash."

Two days later, as scheduled, a makeshift crew from the Oklahoma Department of Wildlife works to retrieve a large unidentified object from the bottom of Founder's lake. The team trucked in an electric-drive wench from Texas and mounted it on a 25-foot barge. Two divers are now underwater, securing the mystery wreckage with grappling hooks.

Mayor Ben Thomas, standing on the pier, looks on as Janet Sparks approaches him, carrying a file folder.

"Morning, mayor," she says, handing him the file. "Some talking points for your press conference tomorrow. Looks like we're all set."

"Thanks," he replies, glancing inside.

Janet stares absently at a cluster of dead, bloated catfish bobbing around the pier's pylons. "There's also a copy of the article I sent to the St. Louis newspaper. Remember the story you got so worked-up about? '*Life Gets Dark in Medicine Park?*'"

"I thought we were done with that," the mayor replies.

"It's not the same piece. The difference is, it depicts your efforts to get to the bottom of things in a favorable light. The editor might be calling you to confirm some details. His name's Scott Cunningham. I wrote it down for you."

"Jeez Louise! Can't I stop 'em from running it?"

"*You want them to.* It'll get picked up by the wire services and you'll get national coverage. Great for your career. Isn't that what you want?"

"Yeah. Maybe. I'm not sure I welcome the scrutiny."

"Look. I know there're things you wanna keep hidden. I get that. You're a politician." The mayor gives her a skeptical look. "Ben, we've *all* done things we'd like to hide. We *all* have secrets. But sometimes, events beyond our control…force them to the surface. Best be prepared when it happens."

"So, you're telling me I should straighten up a bit before the cleaning crew arrives."

Janet smiles. "Yes. Exactly."

In the distance, a worker on the barge shouts, "Ready to hoist! Stand by!"

The on-board wench whirs and grinds as both divers surface. "Here it comes!" shouts the supervisor, steadying the cable as it spools. Suddenly, a muddy, rusted object rises to the surface.

"*What is that?*" Janet says, confounded by the dilapidated yellowish hulk.

The mayor squints, trying to make it out. "It's, a, it looks like part of an airplane or something. A fuselage, maybe *and cockpit?*"

As the shell of the waterlogged craft dangles several feet above the water, Janet and Mayor Thomas can now see two large, red words displayed across its side:

"Sky Chief."

The four-story Comanche County Courthouse in Lawton was constructed in 1931. Described by its architect as 'classic revival-style,' it appears more like a concrete bunker with a medieval, castle-style decorative crown. Inside, its austere institutional lobby features black & white photos paying homage to Oklahoma's depression-era oilfield heyday. Oversized images of rigs, derricks, pipelines, and drilling equipment convey an overwhelming sentiment: Gusher!

Today, however, inside the courthouse's expansive top floor boardroom, the primary sentiment is: Anticipation.

Medicine Park mayor, Ben Thomas, stands at a podium facing 30-odd onlookers – a combination of county officials, newspapermen, and concerned citizens from across the region. At the back of the room, two TV cameras –

one from Lawton station KSWO, and one from KFDX in Wichita Falls – are pointed at the mayor.

Janet Sparks and Betty Allen stand to the mayor's right, providing moral support as he addresses the gathering. "Good afternoon," the mayor says, forcing a smile. "Thanks for coming. I'll make this as quick as possible." He pauses to catch his breath.

"There's been a lot of concern and speculation about the recent tragedy on Founder's lake. Which, by the way, was named for my grandfather and founder of Medicine Park, John Elmer Thomas. So, I take a personal interest in what's happened there."

The mayor glances over to Janet, who maintains her encouraging demeanor. "Thankfully, we finally have a handle on it. Last Thursday, a crack team from our state's wildlife department identified what killed over a million of our fish."

The mayor pulls an index card from his jacket pocket and consults it. "It's a chemical called '*Trichloroethane*.'" He looks up and smiles. "And, believe it or not, that's the short version." A few in the crowd chuckle. "Anyway, it's part of a compound that's used to make DDT. Which, most of you know, is a pesticide. And from what I'm told, it's highly toxic. It was used by one of our local crop dusters. Many of you know his name: Sampson Whitefeather…Chief Quanah Parker's great grandson."

There's a faint murmur among the audience. "Last Thursday, the wildlife team pulled the wreckage of Whitefeather's plane from the bottom of the lake. They think it's been down there since mid-June, when the tornado came through and blew his aircraft from the sky. Completely shattered most of it. The only part of his craft that made it to the bottom contained the cockpit and storage hopper underneath it filled with nearly 200 gallons of DDT."

He pauses to let this sink in. "The wildlife department tells me the poison probably stayed inside the hopper for months, till early November, when the welds ruptured and the chemical finally spilled out. It took about 10 days after that for the dead fish to bloat 'n' float. No signs of Sampson's body remain. We did, however, find his pearl-handled hunting knife, wedged into a corner of the cockpit door."

He adjusts the knot on his bright green tie. "Okay. So, the good news is, we finally have closure on former Lieutenant Whitefeather. He's entombed in the lake. But there's *bad news* from all this. Restoring the lake will take time.

We don't know how long. It involves dredging, planting, filtering, frankly, this is new to all involved. Suffice it to say, Founder's Lake will be closed to the public until we can sort it all out. It'll probably be a good while. I wish there was another way."

"Okay. I'll open it up for questions." Vic Chandler, standing among the attendees, raises his hand. The mayor recognizes him. "Yes, you in the back."

"Vic Chandler from the Gazette."

"Yes, Vic."

"So, Mr. Mayor, speaking of tragedies, we've had a vicious murder in Medicine Park. And the killer's still at large. Could you comment on the state of the investigation at this point?"

"Well, first, you all probably know last month, our high school football coach and long-time resident, Carter Singleton, was gruesomely dismembered. I hesitate to get too graphic, with TV viewers looking on. I'll say this: while we've found his right hand and left leg, the rest of his body is still at large. And, like you indicated, Vic, so is the killer."

Janet, moving even closer to Thomas, jumps in. "Mr. Mayor, we're all pretty frightened that this killer is still out there somewhere, and we have no idea how, or where, he'll strike next. What can we, as citizens, do to help?"

"Well, there's *a lot* folks can do." He looks directly to the cameras in the back. "Those of you out there watching, please, we need your eyes and ears. If you know *anything*, no matter how small, if you've seen or heard something suspicious, if you have *any* information that can help us find this violent killer, call our law enforcement team at 232–4677 in Medicine Park. Once again, that's 232–4677."

The mayor, with fire in his eyes, hits his stride. "Call us anytime, day, or night! We're depending on you for help. *Let's bring this killer home for Christmas!*"

The following day, Janet stands outside the Gazette newspaper office watching Vic Chandler through the storefront window. He sits behind the corner desk, packing its contents into a cardboard box. He looks up to see her, flashes a big smile and beckons her inside.

"Hey, what brings you to town?" Vic says as Janet gently closes the door behind her.

"I brought you a present," she replies, pulling a small wrapped box from her purse. "It's a thank-you for all you've done for me."

"What have I done?" he replies, waving her off.

"The typewriter. The camera. The moral support. I could go on."

"Okay, okay. I'm a great guy. But you shouldn't have."

Janet lays the box on the desk. "Go ahead. Open it."

"Can I wait for a special occasion?"

"Like what? Christmas?"

"Or dinner. I'd invite you out, but I cook better than anyone around here. So, come to *my house*. For grilled rainbow trout. And I toss a mean salad."

"Hmm. Okay. When?"

"Tomorrow night?"

"I'll have to check with Jonny. To see if he needs the car."

Vic chuckles. "Tell you what: *I'll* pick you up. My house is hard to find, anyway."

Janet considers this as Vic scrutinizes her giftwrap. "Okay," Janet replies, hesitantly. "But I'm a little embarrassed by where I live." Vic gives her a questioning look. She blushes. "My parent's house. Their *run-down* house."

"No worries. Make it 6:30. It'll be pitch dark by then and I'll only see a hint of the ugly shack."

Janet laughs. "Good. *I feel so much better now.*"

The following night, as Jonny drives to Bren Lace's house in the family Chevy, Janet waits at her front door for Vic to arrive. "I hope he ignores this place," she thinks to herself, wishing her parents had kept it up.

Vic finally pulls up, parking under the streetlight on Merry Circle Drive. He emerges from the driver's seat of what appears to be – to Janet's eyes – an exotic sports car.

"Like it?" Vic asks as Janet admires it from the porch.

"Lovely," Janet replies, walking toward the car. "What is it?"

"A '52 Porsche Roadster. It's my baby but it costs too much to drive."

"Well, that's practical," Janet replies. Vic opens the passenger door and Janet, wearing a gray wool skirt, tries her best to gracefully slide into its tiny cockpit. Moments later, as Vic fires up the engine and she hears its throaty roar, she makes a mental note that she's tired of being practical.

"Ever been up to Mount Scott?" Vic asks, maneuvering his silver 356 Roadster along East Lake Road, south of the town's main drag, and merging onto two-lane Highway 49.

"No," Janet replies, enjoying the vibration of the car's undercarriage.

"The turnoff's just past Founder's Lake," he says as they continue west. "Right before we reach the Wichita Mountains."

Moments later, Vic makes a hard right at the barely-visible Mount Scott exit. He drives aggressively, constantly up-and-downshifting along the winding, four-mile corkscrew road that leads to the summit. "I'm sure it's a great view," Janet says, enjoying the ride. "But it's so dark, I can't see anything."

"It's tremendous!" Vic replies. "My house overlooks Lake Lawtonka. But the best part is very few neighbors." Vic makes a quick left turn, whipping the Porsche up a steep, narrow driveway. He makes an abrupt stop beneath a side carport. The house lights immediately pop on, revealing Vic's modern, mid-century home on their left. Its steep, V-shaped roof dramatically frames the dark brick and glass front entryway.

Janet tries to discern the contours of the house through the front windshield. Vic shuts off the engine and turns to her. "The architect installed the automatic lights, some kind of motion-sensor hocus-pocus. In fact, he custom-built *everything*. He planned to live here himself." Vic flashes an ironic smile. "That was before he was sentenced to five years for embezzlement."

Later that evening, Jonny & Bren sit together on the piano bench in the corner of her living room. She turns to him. "It's the first time I've used an A major 7th and C sharp minor in a song. Makes for a great melody, I think."

"What's it about?" Jonny says, gazing at her scrawled notebook notations, propped on the ledge of her vintage upright Davenport piano.

"Well, remember when you told me about lying awake at night, in St. Louis? And wondering if there was someone out there who was right for you? That perfect person?"

"Yeah," Jonny replies, embarrassed at the thought of having shared that with her.

"So, I wrote some lyrics around the line, '*I Wonder Where You Are Tonight.*'"

"Hmm. Sounds good," Jonny replies. "Play it for me."

Bren takes a deep breath. "Okay. There's a line or two I need some help with."

"Sure. If I can."

Bren plays a melodic intro to her song, then dives into the lyrics with the best voice she can summon:

> Some things are hard to learn…
> Some fly over my head.
> Can't believe half the things I've said.
> Sometimes my mind talks back.
> Tells me I'll always be on my own.
> All I know, I'm tired of being alone.
> I wonder where you are tonight
> Hope you're looking for me
> I know there's someone out there – for me.

She looks expectantly to Jonny as she vamps with C-sharp minor, D minor and E chords. "Here's where I need a line…"
> "Da-da-da-da-da-da-dah…Da-da-da-da-da-da."

Jonny thinks as she continues her holding pattern. Finally, he ventures,

> "Someday I might get it right, good things coming to me…"

Bren nods as she jumps in to complete the line:

> I know there's someone out there – for me!
> I wonder where you are tonight

Wonder where you are tonight
Wonder where you are tonight.

"And that last line fades out," Bren says, giving Jonny an expectant look. "Well, that's it. It needs another verse but whaddaya think?"

"It's great. I love it. But, it's too good for *Thin Ice*. We couldn't do it justice. Maybe the Everly Brothers. Or Gene Pitney."

"Well, *that's* not gonna happen. At least no time soon."

"What about the one you wrote last week, the dance song?"

"You mean *Come on Baby, Dance with Me?*"

"Yeah! We should work *that one* up. It's perfect for us."

Bren's father, Herman, crosses from the kitchen into the living room holding a large tumbler filled with liquid spirits. The ice cubes clink loudly. "Hi, Jonny. Sounded nice, Bren. I think Steve and Eydie are in trouble."

"Hi, Mr. Lace," Jonny replies, glancing at Herman, then back to the piano keys.

"Ready for your last day of school tomorrow, Jon? Before the holidays kick in?"

"Yeah, sure. I guess so."

Herman's just getting started. "It's the end of the line for Medicine Park High. The coffin nail."

"Dad, stop," Bren replies, trying to motivate her father's quick exit. Jonny shrugs, flashing Herman a tolerant smile.

"Me? I plan to take next year off," Herman says, pressing on. "Maybe write the *real* story of this town. Might call it '*Bad Medicine.*'"

"I'm, uh, not sure what you mean," Jonny replies, clandestinely squeezing Bren's hand under the keyboard.

"Well, it goes *this* way," Herman grins, relishing this. "While the hopeful citizens await the mayor's promise of new schools and shopping centers and financial nirvana. His Honor has bigger fish to fry." Herman takes a big gulp from his tumbler. "See, Ben Thomas and his 'silent partners' a.k.a. top army officers at Fort Sill are buying up swaths of land between here and Elgin. Cheap, fallow land. But you don't need rich dirt when your plans involve *pay-dirt* horse racing and the gambling money that comes with it."

"That's just your opinion, Dad," Bren interjects, embarrassed by Herman's diatribe. Jonny stares patiently at Herman, his fingers reflexively tapping the piano keys.

"If you're following me, Jonny, you realize the metaphor here is a school of dead fish floating on a lake. Teachers, shopkeepers, plumbers, watching town commerce drift east, becoming another town's reward. Elgin's commissioner looks the other way. Incorporated land meets bribery incorporated. Illegal gambling rules the roost, an extension of what goes on every day at the mayor's club."

Bren winces as Herman savors another swig, the ice clinking louder. "I wish you'd cut down on your drinking, Daddy."

Herman pretends not to hear as he gathers steam. "All due, ya understand, to the poison beneath the lake: Mayor Ben Thomas." He chuckles. "And you know what? Coach Singleton was on to the whole thing. He threatened to blow the whistle for a piece of the action. *And look how that turned out!*"

Bren and Jonny stare at each other, eyes wide. Bren's heard her father's conspiracy theories many times before, but this one's the capper.

Vic and Janet sit together in his dining room, savoring fresh grilled trout and baked russet potatoes. Janet gazes into the adjacent kitchen, envious of its built-in, stainless-steel appliances, and custom granite countertops.

"You haven't mentioned a word about your hotline calls," Vic says, guiding his fork to his salad bowl.

"You mean, tips on Coach Singleton's murder?" Vic nods. "Well, I'm not sure it's good dinner conversation. Let's just say, the crazies are coming out of the woodwork. I've had a few interesting leads, though that I passed on to the sheriff."

"You started to mention a call from Herman Lace."

"Oh, yeah. His was the nuttiest. Or *maybe not.*" Janet savors the last bite of her trout. "Vic, how well do you know Ben Thomas?"

"I'm not sure *anyone* knows him. He keeps his family hidden away. His kids go to some Christian Academy in Lawton. Don't know anyone who's been to his house. Or his *estate*, I should say."

Janet considers this. "He's a strange bird."

"Fair to say." He smiles. "Can I mix you another drink?"

Janet hoists her cocktail glass. "What'd you call this? A Manhattan?"

"Right. Nectar of the Gods…"

"Yes, please," Janet replies, handing Vic her glass. He crosses to the liquor cabinet near the brick fireplace, built into the back wall of his sparsely furnished living room. "I took the liberty of opening your gift," he calls out.

"You what?" Janet replies, carrying empty plates and salad bowls to the kitchen.

"I can always use a pen and pencil set, especially from Parker. They're made to last."

Janet crosses to the living room to assist with the drinks. "It's the only brand I could find in Lawton," she replies. "Forget Tiffany's."

"I appreciate it," Vic assures her, handing her two ice-filled glasses. "Thank you."

"Speaking of taking liberties," Janet says, watching him pour splashes of Canadian Club. "Earlier, on my way to the bathroom, I peeked in your office. You've got a lot of books!"

"Well. Yeah. Astronomy's a hobby of mine," he replies, dribbling out portions of sweet Vermouth.

"That doesn't explain the law books or the diploma on the wall beside the light switch." Vic gives her an appraising look. Janet smiles at him. "You could do a better job of hiding it."

His eyes widen. "Or I could be more careful who I invite over."

Janet leans back, taking his measure. "SMU, huh? In Dallas. Aren't we fancy!"

Vic chuckles. "*I know* you're teasing."

"How come you never mentioned it?"

Vic stirs both drinks with a swizzle stick. "I told you, I had a business in Oklahoma City."

"You did, yes."

"It was a law firm. I was a defense attorney. Some criminal, mostly corporate executive stuff." Vic motions for her to join him on the tan leather sofa near the picture window.

Janet hoists her glass in a mock toast. "I could be wrong but you seem to have done quite well. Congratulations."

Vic's hesitant. "Yeah. Things were good for well, quite a while, actually." Vic swishes ice around in his glass. "I had two partners. One was my wife…until she died of leukemia. That's what broke up the band."

"That must've been awful," Janet replies, thinking of her own family tragedy.

"*It was*. At the time, it seemed like a never-ending hell." Vic reflects on this. "But you get down the road a few years you look back, and it seems like it happened quickly." Janet's intrigued, and she waits for him to continue. "Time's funny like that, you know. You get to my age, it plays tricks. It's not so linear anymore. It's more elastic."

"Whaddaya mean by elastic?"

"It expands and contracts, depending on how you perceive things, the situation you're in and the opportunities in front of you. Time can even start to bend."

"I'm not sure what you mean."

"Take *you*, Janet. Betty told me when you first came here, you were practically paralyzed with grief. But after watching you these past weeks, I've seen someone whose life arc is *bending* toward new possibilities. Time's becoming your friend again. And it suits you."

Janet blushes. "Vic, that's the sweetest – *and most bewildering* – thing anyone has ever said to me. I suppose I should thank you."

"Not necessary." Vic smiles. "But I *do accept* hugs."

Once again, she blushes, masking how seriously she considers his offer.

Later that evening, Jonny is in his bedroom, door closed. He attempts to watch *The Tonight Show with Johnny Carson* through waves of interference on the portable black & white Zenith perched on his dresser drawer. He adjusts the built-in rabbit ears behind the set, only slightly improving the blurry images. He makes a mental note to add television reception to the list of things he misses about St. Louis.

He hears a knock on the door, followed by his mother's voice: "Jonny, you home already?"

"Come in," he replies over the televised audience laughter.

Janet cracks the door open and pokes her head in. "Did you and Bren have a good time tonight?"

Jonny lowers the volume, then plops down on the foot of his bed. "Sort of. We went to a drive-in, in Lawton. But Bren's old boyfriend, Dale Collins, pulled in next to us, with a date. We tried to ignore him, but Bren got kinda bummed. So, I took her home."

"Oh. That's too bad," Janet replies, stepping into the room.

"Sometimes this place gets to me," Jonny says, frustrated. After a moment of moody silence, he continues. "I dunno, Mom. It's like, everybody knows everybody around here. You can't go *anywhere* without running into somebody you don't wanna see."

Janet smiles, knowingly. "I guess it's part of the Medicine Park charm."

Jonny considers this. "Too many people here have a sad past. And a worse future. It depresses me." He forces a smile. "Anyway, how was *your* date?"

Janet's eyes light up. "I had dinner tonight with a man who has a different take on all that. *He believes*, if we could escape yesterday's hurts and regrets, and our fear and anxiety about tomorrow, we'd discover that the past, the present and the future all exist at the same time. And it's the ideal place to be." She smiles. "That's a great thought, don't you think?"

Jonny gives her a long, searching look, trying to make sense of it. "Mom, have you been drinking?"

Janet, as usual, is having difficulty falling asleep. Part of the reason: a nightly realization that she's back in her childhood bedroom, with the ghost of her parents looming across the hall. The thought disturbs her.

Even worse, she frequently hears the plaintive trill of a whooping crane outside her window, and she wonders if it's the one who embodied her mother's presence on that strange Halloween night. Of course, she reasons, it's her mind playing tricks on her – as it does more and more often since her return to Medicine Park.

Now, tonight, after what seems like hours of tossing and turning, Janet's mind returns to her dinner with Vic Chandler, and the feel of his hand squeezing hers toward the end of the evening. It was strong and sturdy, yet so soft and gentle. She supposed that years of printer's ink stains and rough metal press runs couldn't reverse earlier decades of white-collar pampering.

She let her mind roam free. How did Vic's hands differ from her former husband's? Richard's were also soft, but his touch had grown clumsy and indifferent. Vic's hands seemed to know and to care. But how could a limb, a mere appendage, convey feelings?

Finally, on the verge of sleep, Janet imagines Vic's hands touching her shoulders, his fingers gently caressing the base of her neck. It begins to feel sexual, full of adventure and possibilities. She feels a tingling sensation sweep over her body as Vic's fingers ease down to her right breast, gently encircling her nipple – which is now becoming eager and erect. She continues to drift away, entering a sleep-induced twilight – that space beyond time, where the mind inches toward parts unknown, a no-limits zone, both comforting and compelling. It's a welcoming dimension, and tonight, Vic's hands are given permission to explore her. She yields to his touch, boldly guiding his hand down to her inner thigh, letting his warm index finger discover her urgency and wetness. She places her hand on top of his, guiding it up and down, faster and faster, excitement building toward climax and yet wondering why there's now a heavy metal object on his ring finger.

I'm not asleep, Janet whispers, feeling the suddenly-cold hand carelessly groping inside her flannel pajama bottoms. She seizes the hand and flings back her bedspread. She's shocked to discover it's detached from the arm – severed at the wrist – dripping blood. It's Coach Singleton's dead, bloated hand – now flying to her neck and squeezing it tightly, choking her. Janet screams, abruptly sitting up, glancing around her bedroom in the dark, realizing she's no longer in danger, relieved to escape that eerie netherworld beyond time and space and reason and sanity. She's back in her childhood bed, alone with her doubts and fears and run-away imagination. The sun will soon appear outside her window. And she'll be safe.

Cecil Ludlow has owned the 'Stop In' convenience store for nearly 20 years. Just up the street from the sheriff's office on East Lake Drive, it's the epitome of convenience for Roy Smirk, who enters to follow up on a tip Cecil phoned-in to Janet Sparks a few days earlier.

"Merry Christmas, Cecil," Smirk says, glancing around the store, noting its lonely isles stocked with snacks and assorted canned and packaged goods. A row of frozen food and refrigerated beverage compartments line the far wall.

"Same to ya, sheriff," Cecil replies, stocking cigarettes behind the counter. "What can I do you for?"

"Well, you called in with a tip about Coach Singleton. You say he was in here the night he went missing?"

"Yep. That was a Sunday. October 27. Around 7:30. He came in the back door and made a bee-line to the phone." He indicates the booth in the rear corner of the store.

"Okay. Noted. Is there somethin' unusual about that?"

"You mean, aside from how long he spent on the phone?"

"He was on a long time?"

"Seemed like it. I think he made several calls." Smirks stares at Cecil, blankly. "But the strange thing is, sheriff, while he was talking, Buddy Allen came in the front door. Looking for him. You know, Buddy, Betty's brother. The janitor at the school."

"Oh?"

"Yep, and he saw coach was on the phone and he shot right out then, about 10 minutes later, he came back in again. And he waited for a bit, then high-tailed it out the back."

"You don't say," Smirk replies, finally removing his trooper hat. "And what'd coach do, you know, after he got off the phone?"

"Made a quick purchase, then left out the back. Seemed kinda disturbed. Preoccupied, you might say."

"Yeah? What did he buy?" Cecil averts his gaze. "You sold him some booze, right?"

"I don't recall, sheriff."

"Look, Cecil. I know you have hooch in your storeroom. It's a dry county but for regular folk, I look the other way. Everyone does. So, I need to know."

After an uncomfortable silence, Cecil replies, "He bought a fifth of Jack. Like I said, I bagged it up for him and he lit out the back. Never heard from him again."

"Did ya notice anything else? Did you check the lot? Did you see him pull out?"

"Nope. I just saw a real edgy guy. And it seemed like he was in trouble."

Two days past Christmas, Sheriff Smirk still can't get Buddy Allen off his mind. And on this cold, cloudy afternoon – now threatening rain – he drives his squad car east on McIntosh Road, with Medicine Park a good four miles in his rearview mirror. Just past the Stoney Point intersection, he spots Buddy's dilapidated wooden frame house on the right, about 50 yards off the road. Smirk cautiously pulls onto the potholed, graveled drive that leads past Buddy's 'sculpture garden' of rusted, junked cars. On each side of the road, the dead switchgrass and leafless dogwood trees reinforce winter's grip.

Standing on Buddy's creaky wooden porch, the sheriff knocks several times before Buddy cracks open the chipped and rotting front door. Buddy, wearing faded black coveralls, seems genuinely pleased to see Smirk.

"Hey, sheriff! What brings you out this way?"

"Hi, Buddy. I was talking to Cecil Ludlow, you know, at the 'Stop In.' He tells me you might've seen Coach Singleton there on the night he disappeared. Just wanted to ask a couple questions. Do ya mind?"

"Uh, sure. Sure! Come in. Where's my manners?" Buddy opens the door, gesturing Smirk inside.

The sheriff hesitantly steps in, gazing around the front room, noting that it's relatively clean and orderly despite the worn, Spartan furnishings and cracked concrete floor. The walls are blank, save a prominent painting of dogs playing poker. Smirk points it out. "Say, I've seen a few of those. They remind me of the guys playin' *Texas Hold 'em* at the Sportsman's Club." He looks over to see if Buddy's engaged.

"Never been out there," Buddy replies. "Can I get you some coffee, sheriff? Or would you like a beer?"

"No, no. Thanks. But I'll take a glass of water, if you've got one."

Buddy chuckles. "Sure thing. Got plenty on tap." He shuffles back into the kitchen and Smirk follows. "How'd Christmas treat ya, sheriff?"

"Can't complain. I was hoping for a retirement package, but I guess I'll have to wait till next year."

"I heard *that*! You know, with the high school closing, I'm in a kind of *forced retirement*. In fact, that's why I was lookin' for coach that night. To ask him for a job. Thought he might have an opening at Elgin. You know, as an assistant."

"You don't say," Smirk replies, gazing out the kitchen window into the scraggly backyard, where a rusted-out washing machine and discarded lawn ornaments surround a vehicle covered by a worn gray tarp. About 40 feet to the right, Smirk makes note of a deteriorating shed that looks abandoned.

Buddy notices Smirk noticing. He hands the sheriff a glass filled with light brown tap water. Smirk starts to sip, then thinks better of it. "I build furniture out there," Buddy says, indicating the shed. "Don't get out there much when it turns cold."

"You don't say," Smirk repeats, wondering what goes on inside.

"Can I show you around? Like to see my woodworking tools? Don't have many, but what I've got, I put to good use." He beckons Smirk to the living room. "In fact, sheriff, check out the chair I just built."

Smirk hesitates, then follows him toward the oak rocker in the corner of the room. It faces a 20-inch Admiral black & white TV, lying on top of an aluminum folding tray. "Go ahead, sheriff, sit down. It's real comfy."

Smirk gingerly lowers himself onto the hard, oak chair, wishing it had a cushion to minimize the discomfort. "Hmm," he mutters, rocking back and forth. "At least it doesn't wobble."

"I know! Took me weeks, but I'm happy how it turned out."

"I bet your wife loves it," Smirk replies, baiting him. "Is this her favorite, or does she prefer that one over there?" He points to the tattered cloth sofa in the middle of the room.

"The sofa, for sure," Buddy replies, slightly taken aback. "That is, before she left. She's off tending to her mother. Down in Duncan. She's been sick for weeks."

"Sorry to hear that." Smirk struggles to his feet, glad to be out of the chair. "I'm sure things have been tough for you two." He turns to face Buddy. "You did some hard time a few years back, didn't you?"

Buddy's uneasy with this, but he's had to contend with it many times. "Yes, sir. Six years at the State Pen. In McAlester."

"Man, that's the big leagues! The charge?"

Buddy hesitates. "Involuntary manslaughter. It was self-defense, but the jury went pretty hard on me."

"Well, that's a max of ten, you did six. Could've been worse, but that's easy for me to say." Smirk considers this. "Look, Son…I've taken enough of your time. All I ask: if you see or hear anything that can help us track down coach's killer, please get in touch. We need all the help we can get."

"I sure will, sheriff. And I hope you get your man. I mean, Coach Singleton meant a lot to me."

"That so?" Smirk replies, turning to leave.

"Yes, sir. He helped make me what I am today."

Smirk takes a final glance around Buddy's sad and broken home, unable to adequately respond as he closes the weathered door behind him.

It's New Year's Eve at Wilton Tate's mansion on the outskirts of Elgin.

The occasion: The newly formed, Dallas-based Mary Kay Cosmetics company is holding its premier sales recruitment party inside the mansion's expansive first-floor living space. The overnight event is hosted by Wilton's wife, Gloria – who company founder Mary Kay Ash selected as its first Area Sales Director.

Over two dozen ambitious young women drove in from as far away as Oklahoma City, Ft. Worth, Amarillo, and Albuquerque.

The mission: to launch their careers as Independent Beauty Consultants, representing Mary Kay's exclusive line of cosmetics and facial skin care products.

The afternoon was devoted to training and motivation. Now, the celebration begins.

The evening's festivities kick off with a live performance by a new local band called *Thin Ice*. The group's booking has much less to do with talent or notoriety than the fact that Gloria Tate's son, Parker, plays lead guitar and sings back-up for vocalist Jonny Sparks and keyboardist, guitarist and songwriter, Bren Lace all supported by the rhythmic pounding of drummer Blaze Whitefeather.

The musicians and their sound equipment are set up in front of the living room's 50-foot flagstone back wall, with built-in fireplace. After performing well-received covers of songs by Roy Orbison, The Drifters, Buddy Holly, and Sam Cooke, Jonny Sparks introduces their closing number as the appreciative audience gathers around:

"Thank you, thanks a lot! Now, here's tonight's final song, written by our own Bren Lace. It's called *C'mon Baby, Dance with Me*. And it's inspired by a group from England, I'm sure you'll all hear about soon, the Beatles." He turns to the band, "Okay, ready one, two, one-two-three-four."

The band kicks in, playing a driving rock 'n' roll chord progression of D, B-minor, D, A and back to D, followed by Jonny belting the opening lyrics:

> You say the world is letting you down
> Hope running right out the door
> Too much heartache going around
> What good is crying for?

Parker joins in, wailing into the microphone stand on Jonny's right:

> C'mon baby, get to your feet
> C'mon 'n' dance with me
> C'mon baby, get with the beat
> C'mon baby dance with me
> C'mon baby dance with me

Bren adds her vocals to the mix, singing into the mic mounted above her keyboards:

> Try to find somebody to love
> Jump-start people you meet
> C'mon baby, spring to your feet
> C'mon 'n' dance with me
> C'mon baby dance with me

They sustain the final chord, ready to plunge into the instrumental button:

Too much heartbreak going around...
C'mon baby dance with me
C'mon 'n' dance with me
C'mon baby dance with me!

Their vocals and instrumentation build to a raucous crescendo as the Mary Kay attendees give them a well-deserved ovation.

The grateful – and slightly self-conscious – band members make their way 'offstage' as participants begin mingling with them. One of the newly initiated beauty consultants, Melinda Tate, approaches Jonny to congratulate him.

"Sounded great, hon! Remember, way back when...I encouraged you to start playing parties and stuff? *And here you are!*"

"Thanks, Melinda," Jonny replies, still thinking she looks like Diana Ross. "By the way, I know this sounds weird but were you ever a nurse? Or work at County Memorial in Lawton?"

"That *is* weird! Cause yeah, I did but I haven't been in nursing for years. Why?"

"It's just that I was there, overnight, a few weeks ago. I swear I saw you. You introduced me to your dead brother, LaRon." Melinda gives him a startled look. Jonny quickly assures her: "I know *that part* was a hallucination. But you being there seemed totally real."

"Good Lord, Jonny." She chuckles, grabbing his hand. "I left Memorial too early! They're dispensing *a lot better* drugs there now."

Sheriff Smirk sits at his office desk, sipping coffee. Something about the Carter Singleton murder case is bothering him but he can't put his finger on it. He rummages through his bottom drawer to retrieve the case file. He begins reviewing the Missing Person Report that Singleton's wife, Rita, filled out after her initial visit. He re-reads the document, hoping something jump-starts his search. *Something does.* After the query about the make of the coach's car, Rita writes, "1960 Ford Ranchero. Red. License #CC-8863."

Smirk thinks on this. Maybe, just maybe, he should resume tracking the whereabouts of Singleton's pick-up. He didn't exactly kick himself; he issued an APB with descriptions of the coach and vehicle shortly after Nina Whitefeather brought Singleton's waterlogged hand to his office. But after nothing turned up, he moved on. "Where the hell's his car?" he wonders to himself.

His reverie is interrupted by a knock on the door. "*Who is it?*" Smirk shouts, annoyed.

The door cracks open and deputy Waggoner pokes his head in. "Sorry, sheriff…but a reporter from the *Oklahoma City Times* is here to see you. You know, about the murder case."

"Jeez," Smirk groans. "That story in the St. Louis paper's setting everything on fire."

"You got *that right*. The hotel's crawling with 'em. Yesterday, a guy was here from the Denver Post."

"Unbelievable!" Smirk throws up his hands. "Look, Waggoner, tell whoever it is from the Oklahoma City rag to hound-dog the *mayor*. That's *his* job, not mine."

"Yes, sir."

"And Waggoner…get ready to saddle up. We're paying Buddy Allen a social call."

Sheriff Smirk is on a mini stake-out, parked on the shoulder of the main road that intersects the gravel drive leading to Buddy Allen's weather-beaten house. Deputy Josh Waggoner sits in the passenger seat, pulling a pack of Chesterfield Kings from his shirt pocket.

"Mind if I smoke?"

"Crack the window," Smirk replies. The sheriff scans the property in search of a roadworthy vehicle – apart from the array of rusted junkers fouling the landscape. On the rear right side of the house, he spots a large van parked in front of the shed. Was it there on his initial trip out? He didn't notice it, but it probably belongs to Buddy-boy. He scrutinizes the faded brown vehicle and pegs it as mid-fifties Chevy Greenbrier. Smirk concludes it's the kind of shapeless box that blends in, anywhere it goes.

Except for the van, there's no sign Buddy is on the premises. Smirk decides to make his move. "Waggoner, I'm gonna pull up front and knock on the door. If he's home, I can easily talk my way in." The deputy blows smoke out his window. "In the meantime, sneak around back and ID the vehicle under the tarp. See if the license number matches up. But don't touch the car! We need to preserve prints." Smirk searches the deputy's face to see if he's tracking with the plan. Waggoner gives him a 'thumbs up.' Smirk reassuringly squeezes his side holster. "Okay, then, let's move out."

The sheriff, after his third set of forceful knocks, twists the rusted metal knob and the door creaks open. He pokes his head inside. "Anybody home? Buddy, you there?" No response. Smirk methodically cases every room and concludes the occupant is long-gone. He moves to the kitchen and glances out the rear window above the sink. He sees Deputy Waggoner in back, standing beside the tail end of a red Ranchero, the tarp pulled up to expose its empty cargo bed. Smirk's eyes light up. Hot dog! He strides out the back door to join the deputy, who enthusiastically points to the black-on-white Oklahoma license plate. "Lookie here, sheriff, we got our man!"

"Good work, Waggoner. Go inside and phone the DA's office. Report the vehicle and request a forensics team to come out and dust for prints. I'm gonna check the shed. No tellin' what fun awaits in there."

"You got it, sheriff," the deputy replies, disappearing into the house through the back door.

Smirk stands, hands on hips, accessing the scenario at hand. Buddy-boy mentioned woodworking tools, and a bench saw would be ideal for severing limbs. Would he find blood splatters or body tissue? He'd better not disturb evidence or smear prints. Smirk grabs the rotting doorknob and pulls. It's stuck. He pulls again, harder, and this time the door flies open – *with Buddy Allen leaping out from behind it* – screaming like a banshee, throwing his arms around Smirk and wrestling him to the ground. Smirk struggles, but he's pinned and helpless. He tries to call out, but Buddy's hand tightly cups his mouth. Suddenly, Buddy yelps, his grip loosening as he rolls off Smirk. The sheriff, dazed, looks up to see Deputy Waggoner standing above him, wielding a thick broken tree limb like a club.

"Man 'o man!" Smirk pants, face red. "Am I glad to see *you*!"

The deputy grins, sheepishly. "Here to protect and serve, sheriff."

On a cold afternoon in mid-January, Jonny drives Bren and Blaze toward Elgin to meet up with Parker Tate. The radio is on low, tuned to WKY, the Mighty 93 in Oklahoma City. Bren quickly turns up the dial to catch an excited announcement from DJ Ronnie Kaye:

"And now, number one, and the most requested song of the week from the Fab Four in England, *I Want to Hold Your Hand.* Here they are the Beatles!"

Jonny pulls his Chevy to the shoulder of the road. He feels time stop and the hair on the back of his neck tingles. Some strange and hypnotic effect takes hold of everyone inside the car. As the song rings out, the three of them look to each other, trying to make sense of the indescribable.

Bren finally breaks the silence. "George was right. They've reached the top!"

"W*hat was that?*" Jonny marvels, finally catching his breath.

Blaze is more analytic: "The Beach Boys are fucking dead."

Janet Sparks, Betty Allen, and Vic Chandler huddle around Betty's dining room table as darkness falls on her well-kept home, just two blocks south of the Sparks residence. Betty's wheelchair-bound husband Jack eavesdrops from the living room, which is crammed with Early American furniture and Hummel figurines. Throw-rugs on top of wall-to-wall carpeting reinforce the homey touch Betty works so hard to maintain.

Betty's eyes are red from crying. "They denied him bail, it's not fair."

Vic squeezes her hand, reassuringly. "He assaulted the sheriff, Betty. He's a flight risk. But, the good news, they'll bring him to trial as soon as possible. They want this off the front page."

"I can't reach the mayor," Janet replies. "I think he's in hiding."

Jack shouts his two-cents from the next room. "Don't worry, hon. Your brother has a good lawyer, sittin' *right here* with us."

Vic turns in his direction. "I haven't agreed to that, Jack."

"You *have* to represent him," Janet replies. "You're the best around, Vic. You can't let an anonymous public defender do it."

"I wish I had the money," Betty whispers.

Vic smiles, patiently. "Look, I'll talk to Buddy. Based on what he tells me, *if I think he's telling the truth*, I'll figure out a strategy. I mean, we don't know what we're dealing with yet."

"I feel so guilty," Betty mutters. Janet and Vic lean in to hear more. "It's just that after Carter kept harassing me making my life miserable, I told Buddy, 'I wish that man would go away and never come back!'" She wipes her eyes. "I never dreamed he'd think I wanted him killed."

Buddy Allen is being held in a private jail cell on the third floor of the Comanche County Courthouse in Lawton, just beneath the Boardroom where Medicine Park Mayor Ben Thomas conducted his press conference a month earlier.

On this dreary morning, a dutiful jailer accompanies Vic Chandler to Buddy's cell door. "Your new lawyer's here," the jailer says, jiggling the lock with his keys. "No funny stuff, the both of ya."

"Just call me counselor," Vic tells Buddy with an engaging smile as he enters the cell. His silver hair is complemented by a pinstriped, charcoal gray suit and patterned tie.

"Holler when you're ready," the jailer tells Vic, locking the door behind him.

Vic sits across from Buddy, who's handcuffed and stuffed into an orange jump suit. Vic speaks to him in a calm, measured tone. "I assume your sister told you about me. Is that correct?"

"Yeah, she said you're a good attorney. And you can help me."

"Well, *I hope I can*. But here's the thing, Buddy: As much as logic tells you otherwise, I can only help to the extent you tell me *everything*. The whole truth. As painful – and, yes, as *shameful* – as it might feel. Because, Buddy, if I know exactly what happened, I can figure out the best way to play this thing. The best way to frame your story. Do you understand that?" Buddy reluctantly nods. "I need you to trust me, Buddy. *Do you?*"

After 40 minutes of careful questioning, Counselor Vic Chandler emerges from Buddy Allen's jail cell certain how he'll plead in the upcoming pre-trial hearing:

"Not guilty, due to diminished capacity."

Before Buddy Allen's arrest in the Carter Singleton murder case, one of the best tips Janet Sparks received was a phone call from high school senior Jerry Adkins. He was initially reluctant to convey what he witnessed in the parking lot behind the 'Stop In' convenience store the night of Coach Singleton's disappearance. But he finally decided to come forward. After taking Jerry's deposition, Vic Chandler believed an interview with wealthy, Elgin-based rancher Wilton Tate might be helpful to Buddy Allen's defense, considering pre-trial discovery established that Coach Singleton owed Tate a substantial sum of money.

On the morning of January 17, Vic – with Janet Sparks riding shotgun – drives his silver Porsche Roadster east on Porter Hill Road, toward Elgin. This 12-mile, two-lane stretch of highway is the shortest distance from Medicine Park to the Tate compound. (That is, until the projected March opening of the H.E. Bailey Turnpike, a substantial time saver.) Today's rural route, however, pleases Janet, who gazes out her window at the hardscrabble farmland – acres and acres of rolling fields, dotted with cattle, horses, hay bales and rusted windmills.

Vic is lost in thought concerning the upcoming trial, fast-tracked for a February 3 kick off. The District Attorney has selected a prosecutor: local legal standout, Hamilton Decker. Vic is familiar with "Ham," as he's called by friends and associates – partly due to affection; partly to a wide, bald forehead, bulbous nose and porcine stature.

Vic speculates that Ham considers this a straightforward case, relying on strong circumstantial evidence, plus overwhelming physical and forensic evidence found at the crime scene. Vic also knows that as the county's leading prosecutor for over 20 years, Ham is lazy and feels entitled. Although he usually plays by the book, he avoids detail and homework – which means he probably won't scrutinize the fine points of the case or who Vic lists as potential witnesses.

As Vic's silver roadster continues east, Janet is also lost in thought – weighing her complicated relationship with the mayor. Ben Thomas has begun to rely on her, yet she believes he's dishonest and underhanded – continually placing his own interests above his constituents. She's also dismayed by what she discovered during a recent meeting in his office: ground plans and financial analysis for a new racetrack, located midway between Medicine Park and Elgin. Herman Lace was right!

She also saw documents confirming the sudden resignation of Medicine Park's District 3 County Commissioner, Grant Thurman – ostensibly for family reasons. She suspects that Thurman, a crony of Ben Thomas, looked the other way when it came to Medicine Park's business and financial affairs. She also imagines that the upcoming election of a new commissioner could threaten Ben Thomas' club operations and real estate development plans.

Just outside of Elgin, Vic exits the highway and steers his Porsche along the winding private drive leading to the Tate properties. Vic assumes that Tate only agreed to meet with them after receiving a "grease the skids" call from the mayor. Tate's only request was for Vic and Janet to park behind the house and be escorted to his rear second-floor office.

When they arrive, they're aggressively greeted by Tate's surrogate – a lean, weathered ranch foreman who's all smiles and handshakes. "Welcome! You must be Vic…and Janet, right? I'm Robbie Calian Mr. Tate's right-hand. Hope you had a good trip out."

"Calian?" Vic replies, looking him up and down. "That's Apache, isn't it?"

"That's right. Apache for 'warrior.' Which, I must say, comes in handy around here!"

Janet laughs, finding Robbie a pleasant surprise. Until she doesn't.

The foreman motions for them to follow him through the back door. "Mr. Tate regrets he couldn't be here today. He and the misses took a flight to North Carolina last night. To Fort Bragg."

"Oh?" Janet replies, stepping through the back door into a large laundry room.

"Yep. His son Tyson's been called back to 'Nam. It's a last-minute visit before he ships out."

"I see," Vic says, disappointed, spotting the back of an industrial kitchen around the corner from the stairs.

"Maybe I can help," Robbie continues. "Mr. Tate told me why you're here. I was in his office the night that Singleton fellow came in." He beckons them to follow him up the back steps. "Come on up. Let's talk."

Wilton Tate's second-floor hide-away is tucked into the back of the expansive main house. Aside from a collection of six vintage saddles – displayed on pedestals along the perimeter of this 1,400 square-foot office – the focal point of the room is the north-facing, floor-to-ceiling picture window that overlooks the satellite Tate properties: In the foreground, rows of tall hedges separate an Olympic-sized swimming pool from the main barn and horse stables behind it. Just beyond, a trainer jogs a sleek, palomino mare around the quarter-mile track.

"Quite a view," Vic says, gazing out at the main corral near the stables. Two ranch hands struggle to subdue a spirited black stallion as it tries to buck the saddle from its back.

"Yep. We run some of the finest quarter horses in the state. Even Texas!"

"Where do you race 'em?" Janet asks, joining Vic at the window.

"Mostly Ruidoso. At the Downs. But with a new track on the way, the action's coming to *us*."

Vic turns to the foreman. "So, Robbie, why was Carter Singleton here that night? To pay back the money he owned Tate?"

"Yep. Two grand, cash. Out of twelve. Mr. Tate made him sign a new loan agreement. Upped the interest rate." Vic gives him an appraising look. The foreman smiles. "He had the coach pretty nervous."

"Yeah?"

"He threatened to take the coach's car from him." Robbie looks down at the rear driveway. "It was parked right there – where yours is now." Robbie chuckles. "The guy shot outta here mighty fast."

Vic gazes off into the distance. *Who's that?* he wonders, pointing to the cowboy who's now riding the frantically-bucking stallion in the center corral. He sports a wide brimmed Stetson hat, along with a patchy beard and long, scraggly mustache.

"Him? That's '*Yosemite Sam*.'"

Janet smiles. "Like the cartoon character?"

"Yes, ma'am. Stubborn, ornery fella. Best bronco buster I've ever had."
After a moment, Robbie turns to Vic. "You know, Sam was waiting for me near Singleton's car when he drove away that night. He might've talked to him."

"Really? Mind if I ask him a few questions?"

"Not at all." Foreman Robbie glances at his watch. "It's lunch time, anyway. Hope you brought your appetite."

Throughout 1962, the venerable Dome Theater in downtown Lawton was being renovated, and it reopened as the 'Diana' in time for the Christmas holidays. Now, a year later, its towering pink & white-striped wedding cake facade is a local landmark, and its marquee boasts of first-run movies and a full-service concession stand. Never mind that this week's feature – the James Bond thriller *Dr. No* – was released, nationally, eight months prior. To the folks of Comanche County, this is as up-to-date as it gets.

On this cold and cloudy Sunday afternoon, Jonny and Bren sit in the front row of the theater balcony, gazing down at the dozen or so patrons seated on the main floor. Most appear to be young couples or soldiers from nearby Fort Sill. Most are loaded up with popcorn and oversized fountain drinks.

"The next Bond movie's coming out soon," Jonny tells Bren. "Something about Russia. But it'll take a decade to get to *this* place."

"Who cares? I'll be long gone."

Jonny gives Bren a searching look. "Whaddaya mean?"

Bren surveys the audience as a few last-minute stragglers drift in. "Jonny, you never told me what you think about Elgin. Going to school there."

"It's okay. It's bigger, more going on. I like having classes with you."

"The drive sucks, right?"

"Except the days we carpool. But I don't like Blaze eating in my car."

The house lights go down and a preview of the coming attraction *Bye, Bye Birdie* begins on the screen. Both Jonny and Bren watch in silence, wondering why, in this moment, things feel uncertain between them. Finally, Bren whispers, "I didn't realize until I had you in class, how smart you are."

Jonny scoffs. *"Not really."*

"You are! And I keep thinking you're wasting your time there."

"I'm not sure what you're saying."

"*I'm saying* you should be in a better school. A long way from here. Preparing for college. Your dad left you some money, right?"

"To my *mom*."

"Same thing. You've got college money." She turns to face him. "*So get going.*"

Jonny silently stares at the screen, unable to concentrate. He turns back to Bren. "What about our band? Where's that fit in?"

"Look, I love *Thin Ice*. But we need to look down the road, don't you think?" The movie preview fades out and the curtain closes, then reopens, building anticipation for the afternoon's feature film.

Jonny's disturbed. "I'm not sure what 'down the road' looks like."

The theater fills with Bond's dramatic, orchestral theme music, and the opening title sequence begins on the screen. Bren turns and whispers to Jonny. "Remember I told you I got a letter from George Harrison? After I wrote to thank him for some advice he gave me last summer?"

"Yeah."

"He said, 'Bands come and go. Most don't last two years. But if you can write songs, good ones, that's something you can build on. A future that's yours.'"

Jonny considers this. "That's easy for him to say; he's a Beatle."

"Well, for me – I think it's true."

Jonny's focus returns to the movie's opening visual sequence. He watches as James Bond's silhouetted image pivots to fire his revolver toward the audience, the screen filling with a dripping pool of blood. Jonny thinks to himself, "I finally get why people love Bond. He does what nobody dreams of."

Jonny leans over and whispers to Bren: "I have no idea what I should be doing. You know, with my *life*."

Bren whispers back, "You'll figure it out. I believe in you, Jonny."

Jonny impulsively grabs Bren's hand and grips it tightly, hoping some of her magic will ooze out. Bren guides his hand up to her lips and kisses the back of it, affectionately. His gaze returns to the screen, but for the next few moments, all he knows is: James Bond's on an exciting adventure. And everyone else is just along for the ride.

On Tuesday morning, February 4, a television production crew appears in front of the Comanche County Courthouse near downtown Lawton. A well-groomed reporter with shiny, slicked-back dark hair stands before the camera, clutching a microphone as he addresses viewers:

"Hello, I'm Brad Cambridge, KSWO 7 News, coming to you live. This is the second day in the murder trial of Medicine Park football coach, Carter Singleton. Yesterday began with opening statements from both prosecution and defense, followed by the first prosecution witness, the victim's wife, Rita Singleton. She testified that the coach received multiple threats from the defendant – going back over several years."

Behind the reporter, onlookers congregate in front of the building, preparing to enter. He notices them and glances back and forth from the entrance to the camera. "This was followed by Medicine Park sheriff, Roy Smirk, who testified to the defendant's previous incarceration – ten years ago – for involuntary manslaughter. He also recounted what happened on the day of the arrest, when he was assaulted by the defendant himself."

The reporter spots a middle-aged gent with a bow tie and tweed jacket walking past him, and he immediately flags him down. "Oh! There's Pete Banes from the Lawton Constitution. Pete, will you join me for a few questions about what you witnessed at the end of yesterday's trial? Why it was cut short?"

"Yeah, hi, Brad," the newspaper man replies, reluctantly approaching the reporter. He stands beside Brad, sharing his microphone. "Yesterday afternoon, the sheriff presented a series of grizzly photographs showing Carter Singleton's severed right hand and left leg. Some in the jury were upset, *nauseous even* and Judge Perkins gaveled the session to a close."

"What do you expect to see *today*?"

"Well, this morning, we heard testimony from Cecil Ludlow, owner of a Medicine Park convenience store, the last place where Coach Carter Singleton was seen alive."

"And he placed the *defendant* at the scene, right?"

"Right. Look, the trial's scheduled to resume any minute, so I better get back up there."

"Thank you, Pete, wish we could join you in the courtroom." As the newsman walks away, the reporter turns back to camera. "For those of you at home, we'll be back at five with more highlights. Until then, for KSWO 7 News, I'm Brad Cambridge, signing off."

Inside the Comanche County Courthouse, the second-floor courtroom transmits an air of civic solemnity. Typical of government buildings constructed during the 1930s, the room's well-appointed, depression-era chamber is defined by its high ceiling and dark, wood-paneled walls and wainscoting. The chamber's front-center focus is an elevated judge's bench, with the left side of the room dominated by a 12-member jury box. Also to the left of the bench: a station for the courtroom deputy and stenographer; on the right, a raised witness box provides an unobstructed view for the 40-odd spectators seated, on the floor, in wooden pews. In front of the spectators, prosecutor and defense council sit at two flanking tables facing the judge.

Today's courtroom spectators share a palpable feeling of anxiety and incredulity, centered around the unspoken question: how could such a brutal murder happen in our law-abiding, God-fearing community? Their shared, disturbed murmurs grow fainter as the bailiff enters and addresses them:

"Please rise, the trial of the 'State of Oklahoma versus William Buddy Allen' is again in session, the honorable Judge Rupert Perkins, presiding."

Judge Perkins, in his mid-sixties, enters wearing a black judicial robe and a stiff brown toupee that resembles a bird's-nest perched atop his head. He gavels the day's session to order. "Please be seated." He directs his remarks to Hamilton Decker, who sits with his clerk at the table directly in from of him. "Will prosecution please call its first witness?"

Decker stands and addresses the spectators. "Prosecution calls Grover Stephenson."

Grover, seated in the middle of the gallery, rises and makes his way to the front of the witness stand. Janet Sparks and Betty Allen, also seated among the onlookers, watch intently as the bailiff places Mr. Stephenson's hand on the Bible. "Do you swear to tell the truth, the whole truth and nothing but the truth, so help you God?"

"Yes, indeed."

"Simply 'yes' will do," the bailiff replies. "Please be seated."

Ham Decker stands beside the witness stand, facing Stephenson. "Please tell the court what you do, Mr. Stephenson. Your job title, sir."

"I'm the head of forensics for Comanche County."

"And how long have you served in that capacity?"

"Be about 15 years now," Stephenson replies, adjusting his loud tie, which clashes with his patterned sport coat.

The obese prosecutor waddles back to his table and his clerk hands him a manila folder. He returns to the witness stand, shuffles through the folder and pulls out several photographs. He holds one up to Stephenson. "Sir, can you please identify the vehicle in this photo?"

Stephenson gives it a cursory look. "That's a 1960 Ford Ranchero. Red."

"The same vehicle as the one owned by murder victim Carter Singleton?"

"The same. License number CC-8863."

"You and your team dusted this car for fingerprints after Sheriff Smirk alerted you to its location, last December, parked behind the defendant's home. Is that correct?"

"Correct. We dusted everywhere. Thankfully, it'd been covered for some time, so we got plenty."

Decker pulls some pages from his file. "I have here a copy of your report, and some images of the prints. Can you tell us whose you found?"

The county's head of forensics doesn't need to consult it. "Sure. We found prints from the owner, Carter Singleton and a few from his wife. And there was a bunch from the defendant, Mr. Allen."

"Oh? Where'd you find 'em? Allen's, that is."

"Everywhere! Steering wheel, dash, glove compartment. Door handles. All over the rear bed and tailgate. We also found blood on the passenger seat."

"So, could you say, that at one time, the defendant was side-by-side with the victim? Up close and personal?"

"Objection!" shouts counselor Vic Chandler, seated beside Buddy Allen at the defense table. "Prosecution is asking the witness to speculate."

After a few seconds of consideration, the Judge replies, "Sustained."

"I'll withdraw the question, Your Honor." Ham, once again reaching into his folder, turns back to the witness. "Mr. Stephenson, I'd like to turn to the defendant's backyard shed his workplace, so he claims. I have here, a report based on your team's findings." He holds up some stapled pages for Stephenson to see. "Are you familiar with this, sir?"

The witness gives it a quick glance. "Yup. Very familiar."

"Could you please summarize your findings for the court?"

"Well, in terms of prints, we found prints from both the defendant and the victim."

"Just so we're clear, you found Coach Carter Singleton's fingerprints inside the shed?"

"All over. The door, the chair, the woodworking tools."

"Could you describe those tools for us?"

"Bench saw Craftsman, radial arm. Small hand planer. A power drill. From Sears. A few of the victim's prints were on the bench saw. Although it appeared the defendant tried to wipe it clean."

"What else?"

"Well, we found some dried blood stains around the room. On the bench saw, for sure. And a few splatters of human tissue scattered around."

"Whose blood? Whose tissue?"

"The samples match the victim. Carter Singleton."

Prosecutor Decker pauses to let this sink in. "I have no further questions, Your Honor. But I'd like to enter these photos and forensic reports into evidence." Decker hands his folder to the Judge, who barely glances at it. He looks to the defense table. "Counselor?"

Vic Chandler rises and approaches the bench. He takes the folder, quickly peruses it, then hands it to the court clerk. "All in order. I accept the evidence, Your Honor."

"Cross examination, counselor?"

"No questions, Your Honor."

The judge turns back to Ham Decker. "Alright. Prosecution may call its next witness."

"No further witnesses, Your Honor. The prosecution rests."

Judge Perkins considers this and nods. "Thank you, Mr. Decker." He returns his attention to Vic. "Defense may call its first witnesses. Counselor."

Vic glances out into the gallery. "Defense calls Jerry Adkins."

Jerry, a gawky high schooler wearing his best Sunday church clothes, rises and makes his way to the witness stand, self-consciously glancing around the room as he walks. After being sworn in and seated at the witness stand, Vic Chandler engages him.

"Mr. Adkins. Jerry, where were you on the night of Sunday, October 27? The night of Carter Singleton's disappearance?"

"I had a date."

"*Before* the date. Did you swing by the 'Stop In' for anything? The convenience store in Medicine Park?"

"Uh, yes sir."

"Please tell us, in your own words, what you saw when you were parked in the back lot that evening."

"Well, I was sittin' in my car, waiting to go in."

"And you were there to buy *what?*"

Jerry fidgets nervously for a moment, then answers, "Some beer."

"And you were waiting for a customer, inside, to leave? Before you went in?"

"Yes, sir. Coach Singleton was in there, and I didn't want him to see me."

"Okay. Then Singleton walked out the back door, right? Was he carrying anything? Did he seem anxious or out of sorts?"

"Objection!" Ham Decker shouts from the prosecutor's table. "Defense is leading the witness."

"Sustained," Judge Perkins replies. "Please refrain from putting words in his mouth, counselor."

"Noted, Your Honor." Vic returns to his witness. "Please continue, Son."

"He was holding a liquor bottle. A big one, a fifth, I think. And he was walking to his car and then Buddy Allen rushed up, out of nowhere, and yelled at him something about staying away from his sister."

"His sister, Betty Allen, the school principal?"

"Yes, sir. He grabbed coach's arm and the coach pushed him away."

"Then what happened?"

"Well, as the coach, uh, headed to his car, Buddy Allen spun him around and said he'd hurt coach bad if he got near his sister again."

"How'd the coach react? Did he say anything?"

"He was angry. He shouted back. Something about being late for a meeting. With someone named, I think he said 'Tate.'"

"Hmm. Think he was he referring to Wilton Tate, the rancher in Elgin?"

"Objection!" Ham Decker yells from his table.

"Withdrawn," Vic immediately replies. He returns to the witness. "So, Jerry, what happened next?"

"Well, Buddy tried to stop coach from getting into his car."

"The Ranchero?"

"Right. And then, coach spun around and hit Buddy over the head with the bottle he was carrying. Knocked him straight to the ground."

"Did...Buddy get up?"

"He was out. Solid. Coach lowered his tailgate and he lifted Buddy up and shoved him into the back."

"Into the back of the Ranchero?"

"Uh huh. And there was a tarp or something in the bed of the truck and he covered Buddy up with it."

"Then what happened?"

"He, uh, jumped into the car and peeled outta the lot. Long gone."

"Thank you, Jerry." Vic turns to the Judge. "That's all I have."

"Care to cross examine, Mr. Decker?"

"Just a couple questions, Your Honor." Ham lumbers to the witness stand as Vic returns to the defense table. Vic sits down beside Buddy Allen, who's wearing an ill-fitting gray suit and tie.

Ham looks the witness up and down. "Mr. Adkins. Jerry. I wonder how did Carter Singleton, a man of medium build and strength, get such a large man into the back of his pick-up? All by himself?"

"Well, he struggled, that's for sure. I started to jump outta my car and give him a hand. But I didn't."

Ham gives him a disbelieving look, but decides to let it go. "One final question, Son. What did Coach Singleton do with the liquor bottle? The one you say he hit the defendant over the head with?"

Jerry hesitates. "Uh, I'm not sure."

"Remember, you're under oath. What happened to the bottle? Did it shatter? Did it bounce off the pavement? What?"

"It was just layin' on the ground. After he drove away, I picked it up."

"You took it?" Ham replies, amused. Jerry reluctantly nods. "Well, well. You must've enjoyed the rest of the evening!" Ham turns to the gallery with a big smile and winks. "No further questions."

"You may step down," the Judge replies. He looks to the defense table. "Next witness, counselor."

Vic Chandler refers to his notebook, then stands to face the gallery. "I'd like to call…Sampson Whitefeather to the stand."

The spectators, stunned, look incredulously back and forth among themselves.

"Objection!" the prosecutor yells. "Sampson Whitefeather is not only *deceased*, he's not on the witness list!"

Vic turns to the Judge. "He's on the list, Your Honor. He's listed as 'Sam Parker,' an alias he's been using the past several months."

The Judge shakes his head in disbelief. "Okay, counselor. You may proceed."

Once again, Vic addresses the audience. "I call Sampson Whitefeather to the stand."

In the back of the gallery, a slim cowboy in his early-forties rises and walks down the aisle toward the witness stand. He wears faded blue jeans and a wrinkled white shirt with a string tie. His gaunt, weathered face, close-cropped hair, and straggly beard belie the collective memory of the fierce, pony-tailed scion of Comanche Chief Quanah Parker.

As the enigmatic witness walks down the aisle, Janet Sparks turns to Betty Allen and whispers, "Oh, my God, look close, Betty that *is* Sampson Whitefeather!"

Partial Clearing

"To do good, you may have to engage in evil."

> Robert S. McNamara
> U.S. Secretary of Defense
> November 17, 1963

Ten thousand feet in the air, returning to Comanche County after crop-dusting wheat fields near the Red River, Sampson Whitefeather has an uneasy feeling about the dark storm clouds heading his way. Within moments, his vintage Boeing-Stearman biplane is assaulted by severe gusts of wind and a shower of hailstones. He senses the powerful force of a tornado funnel approaching his plane, but before he can act, a flying chunk of ice crashes into the side of his head.

What seems like eons later, Sampson feels his lungs choking with water as he regains consciousness amid a dark, wet void. His arms and legs flail wildly as he struggles to churn his way out of a potential liquid grave. *Is that a light above me?* he wonders, feeling doomed, his oxygen expiring.

Deepness. Darkness. Blankness.

His eyes slowly open. He's lying on his back, a torrential wind blowing over him. His face and neck sting from shards of flying twigs and hay. Shielding his eyes, he looks around to get his bearings. He discovers he's on the bank of a gale-whipped lake, soaked, his flannel shirt in tatters. He rolls onto his stomach, protecting his face as best he can from the punishing wind.

His mind frantically searches for clues to what's happened. "Where am I? Why am I in this ungodly storm? Why am I so wet and cold? How'd I get here?" Finally, he confronts to the biggest mystery of all:

"Who am I?"

The sudden summer tornado that ripped through Comanche County has finally abated, replaced by an eerie calm. The former naval fighter pilot and crop duster has partly crawled, partly staggered from the muddy bank of Founder's Lake to the two-lane highway hundreds of yards north. His instincts push him along the shoulder of the road, his back to the late afternoon sun. Behind him, in the distance, he hears a vehicle approaching and he turns to face it. A battered pick-up truck blows past him, then pulls to the side of the road and stops. The passenger gets out and rapidly approaches him.

"Hey," the man shouts as he moves closer. He's dressed like a ranch hand in boots, jeans, work shirt and brimmed hat. His long, dark, braided hair and angular facial features feel welcoming – even fraternal.

"Apache?" the man from the truck calls out.

"I dunno. Don't think so."

"Name's Robbie." He looks the tattered straggler up and down, trying to get a bead on him. To Robbie, he appears native. Especially with his brownish-red skin and black, shoulder-length hair. "You caught in the tornado?" No response. "Need a lift?"

"I think so, but not sure where."

"Got a name, ash?" A blank stare. "*Ash*. That's Apache for 'friend.' Hmm. Well, you must be Comanche then." Again, no response. "I'll call you 'Sam.' That's simple enough." He gives Sam an appraising look. "I bet you're good with horses, Comanche."

Sam considers this, then nods. "I think so."

"Okay," Robbie smiles. "Hop in the back. We'll take you to the ranch. Put you to work. How's that sound?"

It's a rainy December night near Medicine Park. Nina Whitefeather, serving her young daughter's dinner, hears an unexpected knock at the front door.

She hesitates to answer it, but the knocking persists. She removes her apron and crosses to the living room. She tentatively opens the door to see a rough-hewn man in his early forties. He wears rancher clothes – and with his long black, braided hair, he looks to be native. Nina's surprised by his forceful presence.

"Good evening, ma'am. Sorry to bother you. My name's Robbie Calian." Nina stares at him, blankly. Robbie smiles, trying his best to put her at ease. "Someone I work with gave me this address, says he doesn't know why, but he wants whoever lives here to have this." He offers her a letter-sized white envelope.

Nina hesitates, then takes it from him. She stares at it, curiously. "Who is this from?"

"That's all I'm supposed to say. Wish I could say more. I think he was in a bad accident a few months back. Maybe he'll remember more one of these days, seems like things fade in and out." Robbie tips his hat. "Anyway, nice to meet you, whoever you are."

He turns and quickly walks away. Nina watches him for a moment, then closes the door. She blinks hard, trying to process what just happened. She takes a deep breath, then opens the envelope. Inside, she discovers ten 100-dollar bills.

Sampson Whitefeather – aka Sam Parker, aka Yosemite Sam – is seated at the witness stand. He awaits the defense council's next question.

Vic gives him an appraising look. "Now, Sampson, Sam, I'd like your testimony concerning the night of October 27 Sunday, the night Carter Singleton arrived at the home of Wilton Tate. You were there when he pulled up, is that correct?"

Sampson Whitefeather stands near the back door of the Tate mansion, talking with ranch foreman Robbie Calian as the loud, labored sound of a car engine announces the arrival of a red Ranchero pulling into the drive. Carter Singleton emerges from behind the wheel, wearing his ubiquitous letter jacket and ball cap.

"You're late," Robbie says, consulting his watch as Singleton approaches.

"I'm here, so let's get on with it," the coach snaps, joining Robbie and Sam at the rear door.

"Hold it, right there," Robbie says, pushing his hand against Singleton's chest. "Before we go up, let's make sure you're clean." He begins frisking the coach. "Got the money with you?"

"Some of it...."

Robbie removes an envelope from inside Singleton's jacket pocket. He glances at it to confirm there are bills inside, then shoves the package down the front of his pants. He continues frisking, pulling a 0.38 caliber Smith & Wesson from the coach's rear waistband. "Well, look here! You know better, man, bringing heat to a meet-up with my boss. That's bad form."

The coach looks flustered as Robbie hands the pistol to Sampson. "Put this in his car, the glove box," he says. "And wait here till I come down." Sam nods, obediently. Robbie grabs the coach by the jacket and pulls him through the back door. "Okay, dead-beat, saddle up."

Sampson places the 38 inside the glove compartment and returns to the back door. He paces for a few moments, then pulls a pack of Camels from his shirt pocket and lights one up. Standing beneath an overhead flood light, he smokes another. He starts to light up a third when he hears a labored groan coming from the open bed of the Ranchero. He cocks his ear and hears it again, this time louder. Crossing to the rear of the truck, he sees something moving underneath a large tarp. He yanks away the covering to discover a hulky man, in tattered coveralls, writhing in pain as he struggles to sit up. Sampson notices his left temple is bruised and swollen.

"What the...what happened to *you*?" Sampson says, lowering the tailgate.

Buddy Allen, wincing, gingerly slides toward Sampson, his legs dangling over the rear of the vehicle. He looks around, disoriented. "*Where...am I?*"

Sampson leans over and inspects the side of his head. "Looks like someone whacked you pretty good."

"*What the fuck?*" a voice calls out from the back door. Coach Singleton rushes toward them. "Get away from him, slick," he yells to Sampson. "Buddy, get in the cab! We're movin' outta here."

"I ain't going *nowhere* with *you*," Buddy replies, rubbing his head.

"Oh, you're *not?*" Singleton snaps, stepping quickly to the passenger side of the Ranchero, throwing open the door and pulling his gun from the glovebox. He slowly, deliberately walks toward Buddy and Sampson, waving the pistol at them.

"*You!*" he yells at Sampson. "Get the fuck outta here." He points his gun directly at Buddy. "And *you* do as I say, and get your fat ass in the truck. You should know by now, Son, I won't hesitate to splatter what's left of your brains across this nice, clean driveway. Move it!"

This is all Sampson needs to hear: Within a heartbeat, he leaps into the air, attacking the coach like a fighter pilot on a bombing mission. Both men sprawl onto the driveway, wrestling back and forth until the sound of a gunshot rings out.

As Buddy cautiously approaches the two limp bodies, Sampson rolls onto his back and whispers, "I think he's *dead*."

"You think what?"

Sampson leans over and places his index finger on the coach's carotid artery. He turns to Buddy. "Whoever you are, you need to get this guy outta here. Fast."

Buddy's still reeling. "You want me to *what*?"

Sampson staggers to his feet. He grabs the pistol from the ground and hands it to Buddy. "I'll help you get him in the truck. Don't care what you do with him. Just make sure he disappears."

"So, Mr. Whitefeather, did you ever see the defendant again, *after* he drove away with the body?"

"No, not till today."

"Well, it's a good thing you moved so quickly that night, to defend yourself."

"Objection!" the prosecutor shouts. "Pure conjecture, Your Honor."

"Sustained. Please rephrase, councilor."

"Withdrawn. No further questions, Your Honor." Vic turns to the prosecutor's table. "Your witness."

As Vic returns to his seat beside the defendant, prosecutor Decker slowly rises and shuffles to the witness stand. He strokes his chin, seemingly lost in thought. Finally, he engages Sampson. "Mr. Parker or Whitefeather, or whoever you claim to be until today, you were some kind of ghost. You'd vanished into thin air. *Presumed dead*, even. How'd you find out about this trial?"

Sampson points to Vic, seated at the defense table. "*Him.* After he came to the ranch to question some of us, I started reading the newspaper."

"Oh? And so, it began to dawn on you, who you really were?"

"More of the past started coming back. Yes."

"Your Son, Blaze Whitefeather, played football for Coach Singleton, didn't he?"

"I, uh, don't know. Do I *have a son?*"

"Oh, for God's sake," the prosecutor mutters. He turns to the judge. "This is senseless, Your Honor. No further questions."

As Mr. Decker returns to the prosecutor's table, the judge pivots to the defense attorney. "Your witness, counselor."

Vic stands up and addresses the court. "I'd like to call the defendant, Buddy Allen, to the stand."

The judge is taken aback. "Hold your horses, counselor." He quickly considers this. "I'd like both counsels to approach the bench."

Vic waits for the lumbering Ham Decker to join him in front of the judge. The judge leans toward Vic. "Are you sure about this, counselor?"

Vic nods, confidently. "Your Honor, Sampson Whitefeather is trusted and respected in this community. There are newspapermen here today and public opinion will be mixed about what we just heard. Look, I'm here to defend my client against murder charges. And I'm doing so under the pretext of 'diminished capacity.' Buddy Allen wants to talk. His account may help the jury reach a fair decision. I'm just trying to give us some options, Your Honor. And I think my client's testimony will do that."

Judge Perkins looks to Ham Decker for his response. Ham's conflicted, but he's also canny. And practical. "I concur, Your Honor."

"Okay, counselor, you may call your next witness."

Buddy Allen sits behind the wheel of Coach Singleton's red Ranchero, trying his best to remain calm after the violent incident at the Tate ranch. He glances over to the passenger's seat, where the coach is slumped over, the front of his jacket soaked with blood. "Coach, I'm gonna take backroads to my place to keep from being pulled over on the highway." He turns left onto NW 4 Mile Road, heading south toward McIntosh. "Hope you're okay with that."

Later that evening, Buddy decides to let Coach Singleton bunk in the rear shed, at least for the time being. Although his wife, Carla, has been gone for nearly a month, she might come crawling back any moment. Or someone in her family could drop in, unannounced, to retrieve personal items she left behind. One way or another, he wouldn't want them to find the coach camped out inside the house – especially in his current condition. So, after setting up a space heater and moving his TV into the shed, Buddy feels confident the coach will feel comfy there.

Buddy's second order of business isn't as straightforward: He needs to remove the bullet from the coach's chest, then clean and bandage him up. Thankfully, the school janitor has become an all-around handyman, and now, as he digs his pen knife into the patient's sternum, he seizes the opportunity to confront him over past grievances. "So, coach, I've got a bone to pick with ya. In fact, I've been upset about it for a long time." Buddy continues digging with his knife. "Steady, coach, this is gonna hurt."

The 1953 Medicine Park Falcons have not only won nine straight football games, they're on the cusp of becoming the town's first Division 3 title holders. Only one team stands in their way: Lawton's all-black Douglass Trojans, who take the field against them tomorrow night at a neutral site – the newly constructed Lawton High Stadium, just south of Fort Sill. Segregated Douglass High is not only a much larger school; its teams have a longstanding culture of winning.

For the small-town Falcons, the stakes are immense, and the team can feel the pressure building as they congregate in the school's locker room after their Thursday pre-game practice. As the players sit on wooden benches near the showers, stripping off sweaty jerseys, Coach Carter Singleton stands in front of the equipment cage and whistles for their attention.

"Okay, gentlemen, listen up. Good practice today! I think we're ready. *Physically* ready. But I wanna talk about your *mental condition*." He holds up a sheet of paper with a typed message on it. "Now, this week, someone mailed me this little love letter. I put it on the bulletin board this afternoon, but I wanna read it to ya to make sure it sinks in."

> "Why show up Friday night?
> We're gonna kick your ass.
> Stupid redneck peckerwoods can't win!
> Soon-to-be champs – Douglass Trojans."

Coach Singleton pauses to let this register with his team. "Now they're obviously tryin' to get inside our heads. So, tonight, I'm challenging you to get inside *theirs*. Here's what we all know: their quarterback, and captain, is LaRon Perry. *He's plenty good.* But not as good as *our* quarterback and captain, Buddy Allen."

The coach paces back and forth, his eyes twinkling. "Now, I'm told their team hangs out at a burger joint in south Lawton, somewhere on Lee Boulevard. So, I'm asking you, Captain Allen, round up some of your teammates for a field trip tonight. *I'm not tellin' ya what to do.* Be creative! But do somethin' to put the fear of God into LaRon Perry and his sorry crew."

The coach anxiously tugs at the whistle strap around his neck. "So, again, gentlemen, *do what you need to do* and I'll see you here tomorrow, after school, for our suit-up and bus-ride to Lawton. Now, hit those showers!"

Buddy Allen sits with four teammates inside a green 1949 Plymouth Deluxe. They're parked in a dark alley, caddy-corner from *Tasty Burger* in south Lawton, watching a group of Douglass students cavorting out front. Buddy, riding shotgun, nestles a cardboard box on the bench seat between him and the driver. It's filled with softball-sized water balloons.

"*That one!*" Buddy says, pointing out a player standing in front of the pack, wearing a Douglass letter jacket. "I think that's him, *LaRon*. What kind of squirrelly name *is that*, anyway?" The guys laugh.

They don't have to wait long: within minutes, LaRon Perry and one of his teammates escort two coeds to a nearby car, hop in and drive away. "Follow 'em," Buddy tells Chub O'Donnell, who commandeers the wheel. "Don't get too close – but don't lose 'em."

"Yeah, yeah, I know," O'Donnell replies, tired of Buddy leading him around by the nose. Chub tails the four Douglass students, traveling in a blue Dodge, as they head west along Lee Boulevard, then south on 82nd Street, paralleling the Lawton-Fort Sill Regional Airport. As street lighting grows sparse and the traffic dissipates, Buddy orders Chub to pull alongside the Douglass car from the passing lane on the left.

Now traveling alongside the blue Dodge, the five Medicine Park Falcons unleash their arsenal of psychological intimidation: As Chub O'Donnell blasts his horn, one of the rear seat passengers, Carl Adamson, shouts through a bullhorn at the Dodge passengers: "Prepare to die, jungle bunnies!" Buddy Allen adds to the chaos, bombarding their car with water balloons. Both girls in the backseat of the Dodge scream as the driver, LaRon Perry, rolls down his window, and shoots Buddy the finger.

"Pull over, white trash!" LaRon yells.

These, of course, are fighting words, and both cars swerve onto the shoulder of the road – the Dodge stopping ten yards in front. Buddy watches as LaRon and his teammate jump out of the front seats and stand defiantly behind their car, illuminated by the Plymouth's headlights. "Five against two," Buddy mutters, acknowledging that the Dodge's backseat passengers are girls.

LaRon points at Buddy, who's wound tight in the Plymouth's passenger seat, and yells, "Get out, jackass! I wanna piece of you   ignorant motherfucker!"

Buddy can't control himself, practically flying out of the car, water balloons in hand. "Have a piece of *this!*" Buddy shouts, pelting LaRon in the face. Buddy laughs, feeling he's dispensed enough intimidation. But before he can jump back in the car, LaRon pulls a knife from his jacket pocket. The switch-blade flies out menacingly.

"Come on, tough guy," LaRon barks. "Show me some guts!"

One of the girls emerges from the backseat of the Dodge, yelling, "LaRon, let's get outta here!"

"*Back in the car*, Melinda," LaRon replies. As he turns to wave her off, Buddy grabs a fist full of dirt and charges toward him, flinging it in his face.

LaRon flinches, rubbing his eyes as Buddy tackles him to the ground. Buddy rolls on top of LaRon and wrestles the knife from him. "Get off me, man!" LaRon screams, grabbing Buddy's wrist and forcing the knife blade across Buddy's left cheek and down the side of his neck. Buddy, furious, loses control and plunges the blade into LaRon's throat. LaRon makes a gurgling noise as Buddy slices his neck for good measure. He jumps to his feet and backs away, stunned by what he's done.

Melinda screams as LaRon's teammate looks on, paralyzed with fear. Buddy, wide-eyed, stares at LaRon, whose neck gushes blood. Melinda rushes to LaRon and collapses to her knees, lovingly stroking his forehead. "Big brother, noooo!" she moans.

LaRon's eyes flutter and close. Melinda turns to Buddy, tears streaming down her face. "You *coward! Monster!*" Buddy flinches, her words burrowing deep inside him. He realizes he's made a tragic, life-changing mistake. And the stinging, bloody slit on his cheek only reinforces it.

It's late Sunday night, and Buddy has dragged his hand-crafted oak rocking chair from his living room to the shed, where he painstakingly built it several months prior. He's now resting comfortably in it, beside Coach Singleton, who's propped up in a metal folding chair. Buddy's new roommate appears copacetic – shirt removed, chest cleaned and bandaged, and his hair neatly combed. They're both glued to Buddy's black & white Admiral TV, on top of the work bench directly across from them. Buddy's pleased that his jury-rigged antenna provides decent reception, even out in the shed.

As tonight's televised courtroom drama, *Perry Mason*, comes to an end, Buddy decides it's time to render a verdict on Coach Singleton. He rises from his rocker and turns down the theme music playing during the show's closing credits. Buddy now hovers over the coach, grabbing the back of his hair and tilting his head up to face him. "Coach, do you swear to tell the truth, so help you God?"

Buddy forces the coach to nod, maneuvering his head up and down. "Good! Now, I need you to listen carefully: The night before our big game, I got arrested. For murder. And the next night, you and the team suited up and went to the stadium, business as usual. But the Douglass team was a no-show. They're grieving, 'cause one of their teammates got killed. And you pressured the league to rule it a 'forfeit.' So, we win the championship, by default. And you spend every day – *for ten fuckin' years!* – bragging how you won the state title. Douglass mourns, I rot in jail, and you prance around with that shiny ring on your finger. *Now, is that fair?*" Buddy shakes the coach's head. "I didn't think so!"

Buddy, straining, drags Coach Singleton, chair and all, toward the nearby bench saw. "Coach, I gotta say, your ring belongs to the *whole school*. It should be in the trophy case, where *everyone* can see it!"

Buddy hurriedly crosses to his workbench and rummages through the cabinets. He retrieves an extension cord and a roll of electrician's tape – then returns to the coach. Using the cord as a tourniquet, Buddy wraps it tightly around the crook of Singleton's arm. He stands back to admire his work, then tapes the coach's forearm to the top of the bench saw. "Excellent," he says, feeling an unexpected sense of pride.

Buddy presses the saw's power switch, then leans down to whisper in the coach's ear. "Jury's in, coach! They find you *guilty for betraying me and for being a selfish prick!*" Buddy grins, mischievously. "I hereby sentence your hand – *and that ring* – to life in the school trophy case!"

The saw makes a labored, grinding sound as Buddy painstakingly guides the blade across the coach's outstretched wrist, severing it from the forearm. Blood, tissue, and bone fly and splatter. Buddy makes a mental note: Next time, cover the bench and floor with plastic sheeting. Oh, well. Live and learn!

Buddy drives his battered Chevy van south toward the school, taking the secluded lake-access road to avoid highway 58. The route, hugging the east shore of Lake Lawtonka, is devoid of traffic on this late Sunday night. Buddy nervously glances back and forth from his rearview mirror to the passenger's seat, where the coach's bloody hand lies, wrapped in a flower-print pillowcase.

Headlights suddenly flash in Buddy's rear-view mirror and he immediately pulls off the road, coming to a stop near the riverbank. He warily watches as a patrol car passes, then slows down, stops and backs up. Buddy panics. He snatches the covered hand and bolts from his van, moving hurriedly to the shore. Glancing over his shoulder, he sees a flashing red light atop the now-parked vehicle. *Lose the evidence!* he thinks to himself, flinging his special-delivery package into the lake. He watches as the hand drifts downstream toward the dam, then trudges back toward his van, making a show of zipping up his fly. As he gets closer, he recognizes the Medicine Park sheriff's deputy, holding a flashlight.

"That you, Deputy Waggoner?" Buddy says, shielding his eyes from the intrusive beam.

"Allen?" the deputy calls out. "Buddy Allen?"

"Yep, one and only! You know, today I realized, I might've forgotten to lock the back door to the school on Friday. I was on my way to double-check when I had a sudden urge to relieve myself. *Call of the wild.*"

"Well, when you gotta go, you gotta go."

The deputy accompanies Buddy back to the van, panning his light through the interior, satisfied nothing seems amiss. "Don't stay out too late, Buddy," deputy Waggoner teases. "Tomorrow's a school day."

"No sweat, sir. I got it all in hand." Buddy winces at his inadvertent phrasing. He flashes Waggoner a weak, apologetic smile, then starts his engine and quickly drives away.

Buddy Allen looks past his defense council, out into the gallery, hoping to spot some sympathetic faces. His gaze is met by frozen expressions of shock and disbelief. The eerie courtroom silence gives way to nervous shuffling, uneasy coughing, and the frantic scribbling of newspapermen. Toward the back of the room, Buddy hears faint sobbing and he immediately recognizes the source. His eyes search out his big sister, Betty, her face burrowed into Janet Spark's comforting shoulder. Buddy glances over to the jury box, where his so-called peers appear overwhelmed. Some look sickened.

Vic Chandler, standing beside his witness, surveys the gallery as well. He notes that Sheriff Roy Smirk and District Attorney Jeb Whitten are not only still present – they've moved closer together. The room feels primed. Vic turns back to his client.

"Buddy, I know this has been difficult. And we appreciate your candid testimony. But I need to ask you a few more questions. I think they're important, and we need your honest responses." Vic looks him in the eye. "You okay to proceed?"

"Uh, yes, sir. Fire away."

"On Friday morning, December 5 last year, Janet and Jonny Sparks reported seeing Coach Singleton's severed lower leg, hanging under the Medicine Creek bridge. Was that your handiwork, Buddy?" Buddy remains silent for several uncomfortable moments. "Mr. Allen?"

"Uh, yeah. Yes, sir. Same tools, same shed."

"Why? I mean, the coach didn't wear a championship ring on his *toe*. No need to transport it to the school trophy case. So, why cut off his leg?"

"The, uh, the day Sheriff Smirk came to school, and he hauled Blaze Whitefeather away." Buddy pauses, bothered by the memory. "Well, to tell ya the truth, I was real angry. They had no right to accuse that nice boy of such a terrible thing. You know? And that night, when I got home, well, Coach Singleton was still sittin' there, out in the shed, like nothing had happened. Just staring at the damn TV." Buddy stops and tries to visualize the scene in his mind's eye.

"Go on."

"Uh, yeah. *I was pissed.* And I figured, if the good folks of Medicine Park could feast their eyes on his fresh, bloody stump, well, they'd have to let Whitefeather go, wouldn't they? It was *the least* I could do. And I also remembered to put down those plastic sheets. Which made it a lot easier, the second time around."

"Okay. So, I'm trying to picture this: the coach's sitting there, inside your shed. And you've cut off his hand. Then his lower leg." Vic leans in closer, locking eyes with the witness. "Buddy, certainly, *you were aware* that the coach was dead? *Had been dead* for some time? Right?"

"Yeah sure."

"Buddy, just to be clear: Do you vouch for Sampson Whitefeather's earlier testimony? That he, in fact, accidently shot and killed Carter Singleton?"

"Yes sir. But I still had unfinished business with the coach."

Vic stares at Buddy, bewildered. "Could you elaborate?"

"I, uh, don't understand."

"What, exactly, do you mean by 'unfinished business?'"

"Oh. Well, the coach never told me he was sorry. About the way he treated me. I needed to hear that. And he needed to say it. You know, for his own salvation."

"Okay, you needed to hear that *from a dead man.* Hmm. Please, go on."

"I decided to keep hackin' him up, bit by bit, hoping he'd eventually come clean."

Buddy sighs in frustration. "*But he was such a stubborn bastard!* Pardon my French."

"So, what'd you do with his other body parts? Once you cut 'em off?"

"There's a deep freeze in my utility room. Inside the house. My wife, Carla, used to put sides of beef in there. It's the perfect place to store his limbs and abdomen. The innards, I put those in the fridge. Thought they'd come in handy somehow. *I sure didn't consider eating 'em.* Don't want ya thinkin' that! I was just saving 'em. For a rainy day."

"Are they still there?"

"Oh, no. No. The day Sheriff Smirk came out to question me, the first time he came out, I decided to get rid of everything. Fast. I threw some parts in the lake. Some I buried in the Wichita Mountains."

"*The head.* Buddy, what'd ya do with the coach's head?"

Buddy chuckles. "That's *my* secret, sir, between me and the good Lord."

Vic gives Buddy a final searching look, then turns to the judge. "No further questions, Your Honor."

The judge looks to Ham Decker at the prosecutor's table. "Your cross, counselor."

Mr. Decker stares blankly ahead, wearily rubbing his temples. "No questions, Your Honor. I'm spent."

Judge Perkins checks his watch. "Well, it's going on 4:30. Let's adjourn till nine o'clock tomorrow morning." He leans over his desk to directly address the spectators. "Now, listen up: I want all reporters present to *stay,* until after the gallery and jury clear the room. I need to have a little powwow with the fourth estate." He pounds his gavel on the bench. "Court dismissed!"

Looking at Jonny Sparks and Bren Lace, you'd swear the murder trial was happening on another planet as they sit together on Bren's screened-in front porch. Bren, her battered Harmony acoustic guitar in hand, auditions the start of a new song. "I haven't written the verses yet…it's about looking back at a long, lost love. The chorus goes from B flat to B flat minor…then A minor, D minor, and back home to B flat, B flat minor, then F."

"Nice! Any lyrics, you know, to the bit you just played me?"

"Here's what I've got, so far." Bren begins strumming and hesitantly crooning:

> "Feelings rushing back to me
> Hints of yesterday
> I hope they never go away."

Her emotions build as she reaches the chorus:

> "How could I forget?
> What could I regret?
> How could I stop thinking of you?"

Bren stops playing and looks to Jonny, expectantly.

"Wow, that's great, Bren." He gives her a knowing smile. "I, uh. Just wonder."

"*What?*"

"I wonder where those words came from." Bren searches Jonny's face, hoping to draw more out of him. Jonny starts to blush. "You know, I wonder if it's *about us?* About you, looking back at what we could've been. Or used to be?"

Now it's Bren's turn to blush. "Sure. I think about it a lot, Jonny. Who we are, what we *could be.* How we met, maybe at the wrong time. Whether we'll have regrets. You know, all that stuff."

Their special moment is interrupted by Bren's dad, Herman, who rushes onto the porch from the living room. "Hey, kids, hope I'm not barging in. Have you heard the latest? About the trial?"

"No," replies Bren, amazed her father can be so oblivious.

"What's up, Mr. Lace?" Jonny replies, knowing it's ludicrous to ignore him.

"The TV news guy, he just said that today's testimony from Buddy Allen was so disturbing, the judge slapped an embargo on it. On all reporting."

"What's that mean?" Bren says, faintly strumming her guitar.

"Apparently, no one can say or publish anything till the judge gives the okay. The court's keeping everyone in the dark." Herman looks to Jonny. "Your mother was there today, right? Think she'll tell you anything?"

"Probably not. Mom doesn't talk about the trial. I think it upsets her."

Herman scratches his head. "Well, from the sound of it, she's not the *only* one who's upset!"

The following morning, Judge Perkins gavels the courtroom to order. He addresses Vic Chandler, seated at the defense table beside his client. "You may call your next witness, counselor."

Vic stands and faces the gallery. "Defense calls Betty Allen to the stand."

Betty, again seated beside Janet Sparks, rises and deliberately makes her way down the aisle, looking straight ahead, particularly avoiding eye contact with her brother at the defendant's table. Vic waits near the witness stand as Betty is sworn in and the bailiff invites her to be seated.

Vic gives Betty a warm, reassuring look. "Thanks for being here. I know this is difficult." Betty nods, trying to smile, but can't. "Just so we're clear, would you please state your relationship to the defendant?"

"Buddy Allen's my brother. Younger brother."

"Would you characterize your relationship as '*close*'?"

"Yes. Considering, you know, we're eight years apart."

"You've been the principal of Medicine Park High for how long?"

"Going on five years." She finally smiles. "Five wonderful years."

"And your brother, the defendant, is also your *employee*. Is that right?"

"*Was.* I hired him three years ago. As school janitor."

"Are you happy with the job he did?"

Ham Decker jumps in: "Objection! How's this relevant, Your Honor?"

Vic pivots to the judge. "Just laying the foundation for upcoming testimony, Your Honor."

"*Overruled.* But move it along, counselor."

"Thank you." Vic returns to Betty. "Your family, they've lived in Medicine Park for quite some time. Is that right?"

"Yes. Since before I was born. My father owned the butcher shop on Water Street for over 20 years. Until he died back in I think it was the fall of '41."

"How'd you describe the relationship between your father and your brother, in general terms?"

Betty thinks on this. "Strained. Buddy needed more from my dad than he could give. I think it's fair to say they were disappointed in each other. My father was extremely hard on Buddy. Sometimes, he'd hit him."

"With his fists?"

"Punches, slaps. Whipped him with anything he could get his hands on."

"Betty, I'd like to focus on a particular incident between the two of them. I'd like you to think back to a turning point, the day you and your mother went dress shopping after school. And you dropped Buddy off at the butcher shop for your dad to look after him. How old were you then?"

"I was 16. I remember, because it was the week before my first school dance."

"And Buddy was how old?"

"Around eight."

"Was he already a troublemaker by then?"

Betty sighs. "Oh, yes. He was ornery. And the *last one* my dad wanted to see that day."

Dudley Allen's butcher shop was within easy walking distance from the main drag through Medicine Park, just south of where Lake Lawtonka flows into the creek. Although it was a small store, it did good business – and most days, customers kept the portly, red-faced proprietor hopping.

Mr. Allen's glassed-in floor display was usually fully stocked, but today at 4:30 PM, when his wife dropped Buddy in his lap, the usual assortment of kabobs, chicken sections, beef cuts, and sausages were well picked over.

Before disappearing into his meat locker to slice some popular cuts from hanging flanks of beef and pork, butcher Allen marched Buddy to the rear storage room and told him to "sit down, keep your books open and your mouth shut."

As much trouble as he had controlling his son, Mr. Allen was stunned when he emerged from the freezer to find Buddy behind the counter, pilfering money from the cash register. The butcher marched his son back to the storage room, where he took off his belt, bent Buddy over a nearby table, and whipped him across his bottom – over and over – until he cried, uncontrollably, begging his father to stop. Dudley Allen responded with another round of lashing.

Convinced he'd made his point, Mr. Allen returned to the meat locker to finish slicing a section of beef flank. He was still trying to get his anger under control when he heard the disturbing sound of the locker door slam shut behind him. He rushed to the door, trying in vain to activate the safety latch from the inside. To his chagrin, he realized that the outside latch had been padlocked shut. "Dammit, boy, *open this door, right now!*" No response. "This ain't funny, Son! Unlock this door. Now!"

It was over an hour before Wanda and Betty Allen returned to the butcher shop from their shopping expedition. After searching the store, then up and down the street, they grew increasingly frantic at the apparent father-and-son disappearance. Buddy, they would soon learn, was hiding in a shed behind their neighbor's house. The elder Allen, however, was completely unresponsive when they finally discovered his whereabouts. Alas, the obese, middle-aged Dudley Allen didn't stand a chance, with his high blood pressure and advanced atherosclerosis.

The night before Dudley Allen's burial service, the Allen family gathered at the Becker Funeral Home in Lawton to preview the body. In addition to Wanda, Betty, and Buddy, the dead man's mother, aunts, uncles and cousins congregated to reminisce and console one another around the open casket.

At the end of the evening, Wanda ushered everyone out of the viewing room, so she and Betty could consult with the florist in the business office. As Betty returned to the viewing area to retrieve her brother, she was horrified to discover that Buddy had snatched the leather belt from the corpse and was leaning over the casket, strangling his dead father with it.

Betty's stunned. "Buddy! What in God's name *are you doing?*"

Buddy, still gripping the belt, turns to her and shrugs, "Nothing…just sayin' goodbye. You know, he wasn't so bad, was he? I mean, I think he did his best."

Vic hands Betty a tissue and she dries her eyes with it. She looks at her brother, seated at the defense table, and mouths, "I'm sorry." Buddy gives her an understanding smile.

Vic pats her on the hand. "Thank you, Betty. I know how difficult that was." He turns to the judge. "No further questions, Your Honor."

Judge Perkins looks to the prosecution. "Cross exam?"

Ham Decker slowly gets to his feet. "I think we need a huddle, Your Honor, you, me, the DA and defense counsel. You know, to get our arms around this."

The judge considers it. "Okay. Yes. Good idea. Counsel, and District Attorney Whitten, please report to my chambers. This court's in recess till 11 o'clock." He gavels the session to a close.

At 11:00 AM sharp, the bailiff and clerk herd the jury and spectators back to the courtroom to resume the 'State of Oklahoma versus William Buddy Allen' murder trial.

After everyone is seated, Judge Perkins addresses the jury. "Ladies and gentlemen, we have an unprecedented situation on our hands. At the beginning of this trial, you were asked to determine, to the best of your abilities, whether you find for the prosecution's charge of murder in the first degree.

"Simply put: Is William Buddy Allen, sitting before you today, guilty of murdering Carter Singleton? Recent testimony, however, has altered the nature and shape of this trial. Specifically, Sampson Whitefeather contends he shot and killed Singleton in self-defense. The District Attorney may consult with the State – to determine whether they'll bring charges against him in this regard.

"In the meantime, prosecution withdraws the murder charge against Mr. Allen and changes it to *'desecration of human remains'* which carries a penalty of up to seven year's imprisonment and a fine of up to eight thousand dollars. Now, with all that said, we've reached a point in this trial where the prosecution formally rests its case, as does the defense. Therefore, I ask you, ladies and gentlemen to retire to the jury room and begin deliberations on this new *'desecration'* charge.

"Now, turning my attention to the press: The embargo I put in place yesterday still stands, and will continue to stand until the jury returns with a verdict. In addition, I order you to clear the building until that time and refrain from engaging with any of the spectators seated here today. I hope that's clear. So, until further notified, this court is adjourned."

It took the jury less than an hour to reach a verdict: They unanimously found William Buddy Allen guilty of *'desecration of human remains.'* Judge Rupert Perkins – taking defense counsel's previous *'diminished capacity'* plea into consideration – sentenced the defendant to three years at Central State Mental Hospital in Norman, to be reevaluated by the state medical examiner near the end of Buddy's term. The judge also fined Mr. Allen a thousand dollars, to offset the cost of memorial services for the former Carter Singleton.

A few hours after the final verdict, Vic Chandler and Janet Sparks visit the Whitefeather home to update Nina and Blaze on highlights of the trial, and to accompany Nina to the Tate ranch to reunite her with Sampson. Vic tells Nina that although Sampson doesn't recall being married to her, he hopes her presence will fill gaps in his memory, as well as help retrieve forgotten fragments from his past.

There's something, however, no one inside the Whitefeather home anticipated: As Vic, Janet and Nina step onto the front porch, they're met by a barrage of newsmen, camera crews and photographers lurking in the driveway.

Their shouted questions and hurled innuendos feel like an attack of cranes, swooping down to devour unsuspecting fish on the surface of a lake.

Vic and Janet look at each other in astonishment; they begin to realize they're trapped inside one of the grisliest stories in Oklahoma's history. Only time will help them escape.

When Janet Sparks returns home from the Whitefeather reunion at the Tate ranch, she's immediately met at the front door by Jonny, who peppers her with questions about the final hours of the Buddy Allen murder trial. Sitting at the dining room table, sharing slices of pecan pie, Janet decides it's time to inform him about some recent family conversations.

"You know, Jon, I got a call yesterday from your Uncle Bob and Aunt Linda."

"You mean Dad's brother in St. Louis?"

"Uh, huh. You know they're renting our house, right?"

"I think you mentioned that a while back."

"Well, they'd love it if you moved back in, back into your old room." Jonny gives her a blank stare, unsure if he heard her correctly. "Linda says she'll enroll you at Clayton this semester. She checked. It's not too late."

Jonny has trouble processing this. "It sounds like you're shipping me out."

"It's your decision, too, Jonny."

Jonny leans back in his chair "It just seems that, I mean, what about you, Mom?"

"I have unfinished business here. In Medicine Park."

Jonny, exasperated, shoves his plate aside. "I don't understand. *What's that mean?*"

"I think the Gazette might start publishing again. And I think the town needs it now more than ever."

"Mom, is this about the Gazette, or Vic Chandler?"

Janet mulls this over. "Both. With everything that's happened, there're stories here that need telling. Lots to write about. I'm also thinking about running for office."

"And Vic Chandler? This is about him, too. Right?"

Janet takes a deep breath. "I think I'm falling in love with him, Jonny." Jonny's jaw drops. "Believe me, Jon, I still have feelings for your dad. But it's time for me to move on. I'm *ready* to move on."

"After six months? Really? *Six months?"*

"I'm sorry. I don't know what else to say. My heart tells me it's time."

"Does he feel the same way?"

"Yes. He says he does. We'd both like to give it a try."

"So let me get this straight, Mom: You wanna stay here in Medicine Park and see things through. See if you and Vic can work things out?"

"Right."

"But *what about me?* I have feelings too, Mom. For *Bren*. I love Bren! Shouldn't I stay and see *that* through?"

"Is that what's best for you, Jonny? As your mother, I don't think so. If you took Bren out of the equation, you'd see what a mistake that'd be. If you think you love her, give it time. Give it distance. Put it to the test. But, Jonny, finish at a good school. Try college. Find out who you really are, and what you could really be."

He wearily rubs his temples. "I dunno, Mom."

"Jonny, I wonder…what *Bren* thinks about all this?"

He hesitates to answer honestly, but knows he must. *"She totally agrees with you."*

Tonight, once again, Jonny has trouble sleeping. He finds it calming to recall the previous October night on Founder's Lake – when he, Bren and Blaze shared the magical peyote cocktail on Blaze's boat. He remembers the euphoria of lying beside Bren, gazing at the multi-colored tapestry of shimmering stars, pulsating like a psychedelic light show. These comforting images lull him to a dream-like otherworld – where he awakens to find himself lying in the dark, on hard ground, inside a canvass tipi. He's wrapped in a wool blanket, sensing an imminent sunrise.

The canvass flap suddenly parts, and an orange glow rushes in to greet him. As Jonny unwraps the blanket around him and attempts to rise to his feet, a native tribal leader stands at the portal, beckoning Jonny to join him outside.

"Come, Jon, daylight calls us to the hunt. Time to rise and take your place among us!"

Jonny, wearing a buckskin vest and leggings, joins the tribesman outside the tipi. In the distance, he sees the dying embers of a large, ceremonial fire as warriors assemble horses for the impending mount-up. Jonny squints into the light pouring over the horizon. "Where're we going?" he asks the elder.

The warrior, his face smeared with colorful paint, points to pine-covered hills a few miles in the distance. "We find many buffalo past there, where the creek flows into the lake, where the minnow becomes one with the spirit of the whale." Jonny surmises that the leader, wearing a feathered headdress, is also a participant in the hunt. "But first," the chieftain continues, "we must create your fierce face." He beckons Jonny to sit, crossed legged, on a blanket a few yards from the tipi's entrance.

"Here she comes," the elder says, pointing to a lovely black woman, wrapped in a bright red dashiki, as she emerges from an adjacent tipi. She looks familiar, Jonny thinks to himself. He watches her approach, swinging a small wicker basket by its handle.

"Meet us at the horses with your brave face," the chieftain tells Jonny as the young woman sits on the ground, facing him.

She smiles, warmly. "Hello, Jonny. I'm Melinda with Mary Kay Cosmetics, here to give you a make-over, using our fantastic line of facial products." She dumps the contents of her basket – various plastic tubes and containers – onto the blanket. She selects one of the containers. "This matte foundation's a perfect start to becoming the real *you*."

"Haven't I seen you before?" Jonny says, hesitantly

"You've met me several times." She smiles, applying beige cream to Jonny's face. "I think we'll follow-up with purple accents. Then fiery red ones, to add layers of fierceness. You have such a handsome face, like my brother, LaRon."

Jonny's confused. "Isn't he dead?"

"Oh, yes. Very much so! Like to see him?" She points to the tipi she emerged from earlier. "He's inside, waiting to meet you. Come on." Melinda gets to her feet and helps Jonny to his. They walk together to the tipi and she pulls back the entry flap. "Go ahead, hon. Step inside." Light streams in to reveal a four-foot-high tombstone in the middle of the dirt floor. It's engraved: LaRon Perry, 1936–1953.

"Today's hunt is dedicated to LaRon," Melinda says, proudly, as they both stand in front of the sandstone marker. "Tonight, they'll place a severed bison head on his grave. In tribute."

"Really? All that because his throat was slit?"

"Well, you know LaRon! He can never get enough blood."

Jonny feels disoriented and he tries to scream. He jolts up in bed, frantically looking around in the dark, feeling a cry stuck in his throat. His pounding heart begins to slow down as he realizes he's safely back in his bedroom. He knows what he just experienced wasn't a dream. Or a hallucination. It was more like a shadow of something real and compelling on the horizon. And he hopes, someday soon, he'll be able to comprehend its significance.

On Sunday, February 9 at 8:00 PM, over 40% of all U.S. families are gathered in front of their television sets to witness the Beatles' highly-anticipated debut on the Ed Sullivan Show.

To those assembled inside the Tate mansion near the town of Elgin, Oklahoma, there was an additional reason for excitement: Patriarch Wilton Tate had just returned from Dallas with a new RCA 'home entertainment center' – a 30-inch color TV monitor, stereo record player, AM/FM radio, and six speakers built into a six-foot-long wooden cabinet. Advanced technology or garish living room furniture? If your household was one of the mere 3% who could receive color programing, it made little difference. The product was amazing!

Tonight, however, the two-dozen onlookers crowded in front of the Tate's new TV console are initially disappointed to discover that CBS, which by then only delivered two programs in color, is airing the Ed Sullivan Show in black and white. But their collective mood turns jubilant as the TV screen fills with spotlights panning the curtain inside CBS Studio 50 in New York – accompanied by a music fanfare and voice-over introduction of the somber, sixty-year-old, shifty-eyed impresario himself.

"*This is it!*" Bren gasps, grabbing Jonny too-tightly by the arm as they sit together on the floor in front of the console. Their bandmates, Blaze Whitefeather and Parker Tate, sit closely beside them – with a group of family friends seated behind on sofas and lounge chairs. Other guests stand toward the back of the room, more interested in their proximity to the fully-stocked bar. All eyes are now on Ed Sullivan, who addresses both the live audience of 700 screaming teenagers – mostly girls – and the millions of rapt at-home viewers:

"Now, yesterday, and today, our theater has been jammed with newspapermen and hundreds of photographers from all over the nation, and these veterans agree with me that the city has never witnessed the excitement stirred by these youngsters from Liverpool who call themselves the Beatles." Screams, screams, and more screams. "Now, tonight, you're gonna twice be entertained by them – right now, and again in the second half of our show." Sullivan waves his arms, extravagantly. "Ladies and gentlemen, the Beatles!"

The curtain parts to reveal the four mop-tops with matching Chesterfield-style black wool suits with velvet winged lapels. Their drummer, Ringo Star, sits atop a dramatic riser behind Paul McCartney, George Harrison, and John Lennon, who strum electric guitars and sing into floor-supported microphones. Following their first song, *All My Loving*, they take a choreographed deep bow, then launch into their second and third songs: *Till There Was You* and *She Loves You*.

The studio audience goes berserk as John, Paul, and George belt out, "*She loves you, yeah, yeah, yeah!*" Inside the Tate home, Jonny watches Bren out of the corner of his eye, wondering what she must be feeling – seeing 20-year-old George Harrison on the world's biggest stage, after telling her, just seven months earlier in Illinois, that the Beatles would soon conquer America. Bren's fingernails, burrowing into the top of his hand, confirm the thrill she's experiencing. Jonny not only senses her joy; he realizes why she's pursuing her songwriting dream so ferociously.

As the Beatles exit the stage, Ed Sullivan returns to address the audience: "Now, they'll be back in the second half of the show after you've enjoyed Georgia Brown, the star of '*Oliver*,' and Tessie O'Shea, one of the stars of '*The Girl Who Came to Supper*.' But right now, a word from Anacin – America's number one pain reliever."

The Tate household, electrified by the Fab Four, must wait a proverbial eternity before the band returns for their final two songs. Many of the guests make a beeline to the kitchen for beverages and desserts. Others mingle beside the bar in the living room. Jonny is pleasantly surprised to see Melinda Tate standing there, engaged with family friends. He's desperate to talk to her, and leaves Bren's side to get closer to the vivacious sales rep for Mary Kay Cosmetics.

Meanwhile, Blaze Whitefeather and Parker Tate converse intimately in the dining room, adjacent to the newly-transformed "home entertainment center," where the Ed Sullivan Show continues its black and white transmission over the heralded 30-inch color monitor. "I can't tell her that!" Blaze whispers to Parker, spotting Bren Lace headed their way.

"You can tell *her* anything," Parker replies, patting Blaze on the shoulder as he turns and heads to the kitchen.

"What's up?" Bren says, approaching Blaze.

"Nothing. Just."

"What's going on with you two?" Bren replies, glancing at Parker in the distance.

"I dunno. I guess we're negotiating."

"Negotiating?" she replies. Blaze shrugs, avoiding eye contact. Bren decides to press him. "Blaze, don't you think I know what's going on with you and Parker? I know you've got a crush on him. You have for *months*."

Blaze is slightly taken aback. "It's that obvious?"

Bren smiles. "I adore you, Blaze. But you're an idiot."

"Well, I know he doesn't love me but…"

"Come on, Blaze. *What?*"

"He says he wants to have sex with me."

"Oh." Bren mulls this over. "Do you love *him?*"

"I think so. Yeah."

"Well…sex can lead to something else. Something more, sometimes."

"You really think so?"

"Well, in *my* case, no but everyone's different."

"Yeah, well, *I'm tired of being different.*"

Bren puts her arms around Blaze and hugs him tight. "I love you, Blaze. We all love you, dear."

Standing beside the well-tended living room bar, Jonny finally gets a moment alone with Melinda, and he tells her about his recent dream, where she takes Jonny inside a tribal tipi to show him her brother's tombstone. Melinda is simultaneously amused and aghast. "How could you possibly know about LaRon and his grave?"

"I don't know. I was hoping you could help me figure that out."

"Lord, hon. I haven't visited his grave in months! What you're saying is so strange!"

"Melinda, I know I'm asking a lot but will you take me there?"

She gives him a curious look. "I don't know, maybe." She sips her drink, thinking it over. "Yeah, okay. You win." She laughs. "But I'll tell you right now, it ain't nothing special."

"Thanks, Melinda."

"No problem. I guess it's time I went back." She takes another sip. "So when?"

"How about tonight? After the show, I have a car. I've got a flashlight."

Melinda gives him an incredulous look. "Jonny boy, *you are one strange cat.*"

Their conversation's interrupted by Bren, shouting from the TV console, "Hey, everyone, the Beatles are coming back!"

The guests hurriedly return to their previous viewing spots in time to hear Ed Sullivan make his big announcement: "Ladies and gentlemen, once again, the Beatles!" Stage lights come up to reveal the four boys from Liverpool as they launch into their next song, *I Saw Her Standing There.*

While Paul McCartney sings, "*She was just seventeen, you know what I mean.*" The camera pans the young girls in the audience, who have no idea what he means, but it doesn't stop them from screaming their heads off. Their heart-felt cries and moans continue unabated throughout the final number – the smash hit *I Want to Hold Your Hand.*

Screams cascade upon screams as the band reaches a crescendo. After taking their final choreographed bow, Paul, George, and John are joined by Ringo, who jumps down from his elevated platform and skips up behind them. A rarely-smiling Ed Sullivan shakes each of them by the hand, and the Beatles wave to the audience and mouth 'thank you' as they leave the stage.

Inside the Tate home, most of the guests are emotionally spent. Overwhelmed. They arrived that evening with high expectations, and the Beatles delivered. Could they wait an entire week for the Fab Four's second Ed Sullivan Show appearance at the Deauville Hotel in Miami Beach? Like the rest of TV Land, they'd just have to wait.

What the overnight Nielsen ratings made clear: 73 million people tuned in to see the Beatles' TV debut. It was the second largest audience in television history – only exceeded by President John Fitzgerald Kennedy's funeral, ten weeks prior. Alas, the birth of Beatlemania helped America begin to transcend the death of Camelot.

By ten o'clock that evening, Jonny, Melinda, and Bren arrive at Highland Cemetery on the outskirts of Lawton. Jonny parks his Chevy nearby, and the threesome enter beneath the west-facing historic stone archway, dedicated by the city in 1936. Jonny and Melinda wield flashlights as they traverse the wide gravel path that runs eastward through the middle of the expansive grounds.

The gravesites are laid out in 20 sections, or blocks, and the nearly 4,000 markers are of different heights and compositions. Some are waist-high headstones; some are flush to the ground. Some are sandstone; some are polished granite. "LaRon's buried close to the back," Melinda says, leading the way. "In a tribal block."

"Tribal? What's that mean?" Bren replies.

"Well, even though the city owns the cemetery, it's restricted. My mom's half Kiowa, so there's an allotment for us."

"That's weird," Jonny replies.

"Well, hon, if you're black, whether you're living or dead, everything's 'separate but equal.' My grandparents are buried over a hundred miles from here, in Greenhill Negro Cemetery. As separate as it gets."

"That's not right," Bren says, shaking her head.

"No. But that's how it is." Melinda points to a distant section with her flashlight. "It's back over there."

Jonny, panning the grounds with his flashlight, suddenly realizes where he is. "Hey, my grandparents are buried somewhere around here."

After walking a few moments in silence, Melinda continues. "You know, when I was a kid, I was taught that we're all children of God, we're one nation, with liberty and justice and all that. And *my heart* wants to believe it's true. But when I look at our schools and churches, our hospitals and cemeteries, *my eyes* tell me it's all a big lie."

"I've never thought about it that way," Jonny replies.

Melinda smiles. "You don't have to, hon. You're white."

She points her flashlight to a four-foot sandstone marker a few yards in front of them. "That's it!" Jonny immediately recognizes it from his dream: LaRon Perry, 1936–1953.

"The flowers are gone," Melinda replies, flatly.

Bren moves around to the side of the grave. "What's that?" she says, pointing to an object lying on the ground behind the marker.

"I don't know," Melinda replies, baffled. "Never saw *that* before."

Jonny trains his flashlight on it. "It looks like a gunny sack or something."

"Is there something inside?" Bren replies.

Jonny hands his flashlight to Bren. "Here, you and Melinda give me some light." He gingerly lifts the sack up and dumps its contents onto the ground.

"Oh my God!" Melinda calls out, transfixed by the foot-long, gruesome, emaciated object lying in the dirt.

"It's someone's skull!" Bren gasps.

"I think it's him!" Jonny replies, kneeling beside it for a closer look. "My God, yes! It's Coach Singleton."

The next day, inside the Medicine Park sheriff's office, Roy Smirk and Deputy Josh Waggoner look on as Jonny and Bren present them with the contents of the gunny sack they discovered at the foot of LaRon Perry's gravesite. The officers slowly circle Smirk's desk, analyzing the decapitated head from an assortment of angles.

"I must say, it looks like he went peacefully," the sheriff ventures. "Or as peaceful as he was capable of being at the time."

"I tried to be careful with it," Jonny replies.

"We'll turn it over to the DA," Waggoner says, puffing on his Chesterfield.

"You shouldn't have moved it," Smirk adds. "But thanks, anyway, for bringing it in."

And with that, the sheriff uses a letter opener to push the coach's severed cranium from the top of his desk, back into the gunny sack, held open by his chain-smoking deputy. "All in a day's work, I suppose," Smirk says, grimacing.

On February 18, two days after the Beatles' second Ed Sullivan Show appearance in Miami Beach, the Fab Four were approached by the publicist for the World Heavyweight Boxing Championship to do a photo shoot with Cassius Clay, the controversial challenger for the heavyweight title, currently held by the brutal, fearsome Sonny Liston.

The Beatles were hesitant to associate themselves with the overwhelming underdog Clay: Las Vegas gave the 22-year-old upstart 1–7 odds; the New York Post predicted a Liston knockout within 18 seconds. The Beatles, however, were eventually convinced to pose with the loudmouthed 'Louisville Lip' – and they met, center ring, at Miami's downtown Fifth Street Gym.

The beautiful, six-foot-two Cassius Clay, in his street clothes, coaxed the Beatles to lie down on the canvass while he towered over them, cocking his arm and yelling, "I am the greatest!" The photo stunt showcased the two most powerful, anti-establishment forces of the new '60s generation, and it appeared in all the major newspapers across America.

The images annoyed and provoked the traditional adult world. Several days later, when the story appeared in *Time Magazine*, the mayor of Medicine Park – Ben Thomas – immediately got on the phone and increased his wager against Cassius Clay. He bet $40,000 on a first-round knockout.

On the night of February 25, the Sportsman's Club in Medicine Park is overflowing with thirsty, testosterone-infused gamblers awaiting the opening bell of the Clay-Liston championship fight at the Miami Beach Convention Center.

There's only one woman in the entire club: Janet Sparks, who sits with Ben Thomas at a dining booth near a TV monitor mounted above the central bar. The back room, usually reserved for poker players, is now filled with fight fans, crowded around several television sets that are strategically placed among army officers and business associates of the mayor.

The closed-circuit broadcast is finally underway – beamed in, via satellite, live to the Sportsman's Club. It's undoubtedly the biggest entertainment event in the 55-year history of Medicine Park, and the mayor can't contain his excitement. "This is it, sweetheart!" he yells across the table to Janet. "They're entering the ring!"

Janet, glancing around the room at the frenzied patrons, tries to mask her indifference. "Ben, I can't stay long. Not that I don't love watching men beat each other senseless." She playfully jabs his shoulder. "But thanks for inviting me. It's great; finally getting a chance to see your club."

"Glad you could make it," Ben replies, taking a big gulp of his whiskey sour. "It's my way of saying thanks. You know, for your support."

"I hope you mean that, Ben."

"Absolutely! You've helped me make some smart decisions, especially warding off those media hounds."

"All I hope, Ben, if I stay in Medicine Park, I have *your* support."

"You kidding me?" Ben gives her an affectionate look. "I'll back you for *anything*, you know that."

"That's great because I've decided to run for County Commissioner. You know, to fill Grant Thurman's slot."

"You're *what?*" the mayor replies, taken aback. "You're kidding! I was gonna run my own guy!"

Janet smiles. "Well, Ben, looks like I'm that guy."

Ben's mind spins as he grapples with this unexpected turn. But his attention is quickly high-jacked by a televised announcement:

"Good evening, ladies and gentlemen!" the ringmaster bellows as a microphone is lowered over the center ring. "Welcome to Miami Beach, Florida and the World Heavyweight Title Fight. Now from Louisville, Kentucky wearing white trunks with red stripes, and weighing two hundred and ten pounds, the former Olympic light heavyweight champion, Cassius Clay!"

The crowd of 16,000 erupts in a chorus of boos and jeers. Clay, impassive, fiddles with his mouthpiece and bounces on the balls of his feet. "And his opponent, from Denver, Colorado weighing two hundred and eighteen pounds, wearing the white trunks with black trim, the heavyweight champion of the world, Charles Sonny Liston!"

Ben Thomas, glued to the TV, is cranked up and ready to watch the destruction of the brash loudmouth, rumored to be a radical Black Muslim. "Liston's gonna murder him!" Ben whoops, turning to Janet with fire in his eyes. But she's already gone.

Within moments following the opening bell, on-lookers across the nation realize this isn't the contest they'd imagined. By the end of the sixth round, Cassius Marcellus Clay proves himself too young, too fast, too skilled, and too hungry to be denied his destiny.

As the warning buzzer sounds to herald the start of the seventh round, the mighty, indestructible Sonny Liston sits helplessly on his corner stool and spits his mouthpiece onto the canvass. *Enough!* Too tired and too hurt to continue, Liston hands his crown to the boastful upstart, who would soon announce he was a member of the Nation of Islam, and was changing his name to Muhammad Ali.

On this historic night, Sonny Liston lost his title and his arrogant pride. At the same time, the mayor of Medicine Park lost $40,000 and his political independence.

Jonny Sparks wakes up at 4:00 AM, thirsty and restless. He tries to get back to sleep, but after many tosses and turns, decides to go to the kitchen for a glass of water. Standing in the hallway, careful not to disturb his mom, he hears a rustling noise in the living room. As he creeps in to check it out, the corner floor lamp suddenly pops on. Jonny jumps with a start, squinting to adjust to the light. Someone's sitting on the sofa! *Two people!* It's his grandparents – bundled in winter coats, smiling cheerfully at him. "Hi Jonny!" his grandmother Ruby calls out. "Sit down, honey. *You never visit.*"

Grandpa Lester chuckles. "No, Son, this ain't a dream. Just a chance for some family time."

"Of course it's a dream," Jonny replies, plopping down in the rocking chair across from them. "You're dead."

"We saw you at the cemetery last week," Ruby says. "You were with two pretty girls."

"You should've stopped by," Grandpa replies. "You were in the neighborhood."

Jonny wiggles in his chair. "Okay, I give up. Tell me why you're here."

"To help you sort things out," his grandmother replies, a twinkle in her eye. "You know, about your future."

Jonny's startled by a knock on the front door. As he gives his grandparents a questioning look, it opens to reveal Vic Chandler, wearing one of his courtroom suits and ties. He clutches a pencil and yellow writing tablet. "Sorry I'm late," he says, smiling. He turns to Jon. "Mind if I join you?"

Jonny can only stare, incredulously, as Vic sits on the lounger facing him.

Grandma Ruby's delighted to see him. She points to the painting on the wall across from her. "Vic, did you notice, Janet kept the picture of Jesus, praying in the garden! It's so thoughtful of her!"

Vic turns to admire it. "It's beautiful, Ruby, Jesus, communing with the Life Source of the universe."

"You mean *God*," Grandpa Lester replies, matter-of-factly.

"Well, that's one way to put it," Vic replies. "In fact, it's what I came to talk about." Vic turns back to Jonny, holding up his notepad. "Ever use a visual device to better understand things?"

Jonny shrugs. "You mean, like *columns* for pros and cons? My dad did that."

"Well, not exactly. See, I think it's helpful to draw an X and Y axis like in geometry. And under the horizontal X axis, I write 'Life Situation.' And next to the vertical Y, I write 'Life Source.'"

Jon leans in to get a closer look as Vic sketches it out. "Okay, Jon, the X axis represents your Life Situation. And it flows left to right – from the past, to the present, and on out to the future. It's chronological. And let's say, you're *here*." Vic makes a mark in the middle of the X timeline. "This is your situation *now*. You're trying to decide what to do – what's the best decision for your future." He looks to Jon, expectantly.

"I'm not sure what you mean."

"I'm talking about the *girl*. The band. College or no college. Do you rebel or conform? You keep wrestling with all this, but your mind's stuck in your *life situation*. You're just hearing white noise both from other people, and the clamor inside your head."

"He can be mighty stubborn, Vic," grandma replies.

Grandpa jumps in. "Wonder where he got *that* from?" Ruby looks annoyed.

Vic grins. "Jon, you can't make good decisions stuck on the X axis. The only way you can make the right choices – for the real you, *for your true self* – is by communing with your *Life Source* up and down the Y axis, a dimension *beyond time*."

"Like heaven?" Grandpa Lester asks.

Vic gives him a patient smile. "More like a field of higher consciousness, where universal wisdom resides. Like what Jesus found in Gethsemane."

Suddenly, there's another knock at the door, and it opens to reveal Jonny's night nurse at Lawton Memorial Hospital – the native shaman – his elder dream-walker. Wearing blue scrubs and a hairnet, he approaches Ruby and Lester on the sofa. "Sorry, I'm late. Busy night in ER. Oh, by the way, Vic, I like to think of what you called 'the field of universal consciousness' as more like an *ocean*. A great cosmic ocean. I think it helps paint a better picture. You know, for the layman."

"Yeah, that's good," Vic replies. "I may use it next time."

"Be my guest," the shaman says, smiling proudly.

Vic turns back to Jonny. "What we're both saying, Son, as often as possible, you need to sit quietly with your Life Source, ask it questions. Listen carefully for answers. Look for signs. But the thing is, Jon, right now, you're trying to find happiness. And when you're stuck in your Life Situation, happiness is elusive. Intermittent. Subject to the vicissitudes of time. But when you commune with your *Life Source*, you eventually experience something far greater: Lasting *joy* which transcends happiness." He gives Jonny a searching look. "Does this resonate with you, in any way?"

Jon stares back at Vic. "So, what do *you* think I should do? You know, with my life?"

Vic considers this. "Well, Jon, you belong to a much bigger world than you'll find around here. Bren Lace figured that out a while back. But you two need to find your place in the world – *separately*. Maybe later, when you're more fully formed, you could merge again."

The shaman jumps in. "Listen to him, Jon. He represents your Life Source. *For tonight*, anyway. Tomorrow, a new one may arrive. Be ready for it! Keep your eyes open, at all times."

"That's so sweet," grandma Ruby replies. "I like that!"

The shaman-nurse smiles. "Ruby, Lester, time for you to go home to return to the ocean." He extends his hands to Jonny's grandparents and helps lift them to their feet. They wave goodbye to Jonny as Vic reaches over and turns out the light.

Jonny sits alone in the dark for what seems like forever. He tries several times to wake up, but eventually realizes he was never asleep in the first place. He just needed to be awakened.

The Oklahoma Press Association clubhouse never looked so festive. Both outside and in – red, white, and blue political campaign signs are displayed everywhere:

Spark the Future!
Vote Janet Sparks
District 3 County Commissioner

Inside the long, rectangular main hall, up to 150 attendees mingle around the lobby bar and food stations scattered throughout the first-floor space. Some stand at beverage tables, some sit on benches covered with red and blue crepe paper. Along the west wall, volunteers man a large table dedicated to voter registration. Betty Allen, passing out Sparks' campaign buttons, basks in the glow of what appears to be a successful event. She turns to Vic Chandler, standing beside her, and congratulates him on the prodigious amount of printing that went into producing the campaign signage. Vic confesses that he had to think twice before taking the plunge. But at the end of the day, he concludes, it was all for a worthy cause.

Their conversation is nearly drowned out by the rousing music of *Thin Ice*, playing atop an 18-inch riser constructed along the far south wall of the clubhouse. The band, surrounded by several Fender amplifiers, sings the Beatles' most recent number-one song in America: *She Loves You*. Bren Lace hesitated to play it, but after a dozen audience requests, logic prevailed.

Following the song, Jonny leans into his microphone. "Ladies and gentlemen, thanks for coming. Now, it's my great pleasure to introduce Medicine Park's next District 3 County Commissioner, a lovely lady, who happens to be my mom, Janet Sparks!"

Janet joins him on the bandstand, aware she must talk fast, and be brief, to hold the crowd's attention. "Like my son said, thanks for coming. I just want you to know that I'm thrilled to have the support of Mayor Thomas, who's probably upstairs, right now, making important calls to bring substantial new investments to this region. And as his partner in government, I promise that a fair share of the revenue his new businesses generate, will go directly to our municipal coffers. To get Medicine Park moving again!"

Janet looks to the back of the room, where she sees Ben Thomas watching from the top of the stairs. He grimaces in frustration, then pivots to return to his office. Janet chuckles to herself as she heads for the finish line: "So, all I ask, if you're not already registered to vote, *do so now* and when you *do* vote, please vote 'Sparks' to spark the future of this great town!"

A wave of applause accompanies Janet as she exits. Jonny returns to his microphone to cajole the crowd, pumping his fists: "Sparks, Sparks, Sparks!" He looks to Bren and laughs. "And now, a new song by my bandmate, Bren Lace, written especially for the folks of Medicine Park called *Our Turn to Dream*." He turns to his bandmates. "Hit it!"

After Bren plays a rousing piano intro, Jonny plunges into the opening lyrics:

Light shining through our window
Running through the open door
Finally feel the wind at our backs
Never felt this way before...
It's our turn to dream
It's our turn to dream!

Parker, with a cherry-red Gibson electric slung over his shoulder, launches into an energetic solo, while Blaze provides a syncopated backbeat. As the music builds, Jonny and Bren lean into their microphones to sing the bridge:

> Try to reach up through the clouds
> Grab a patch of sky
> Now's the time to try our wings
> Time to finally fly

Parker joins Jonny and Bren to ring out the chorus:

> It's our turn to dream
> It's our turn to dream
> It's our turn to dream!

The band brings the song to a climax. The audience applauds, then returns their attention to the food and beverage stations. Betty and Vic approach the stage to congratulate the group, and are surprised to see Nina Whitefeather join her son, Blaze, onstage. She hugs him so hard, he nearly stumbles into his drum kit.

Moments later, as Bren stands beside the dessert table, she's approached by a balding, middle-aged man in a suit and tie. "Say, I heard you wrote some of those songs!"

"Uh huh," Bren replies, stacking cookies onto her paper plate.

"Well, they're good ones! My name's Kirchner," he says, handing her a business card. "With the Dallas Morning News."

"Oh," Bren replies, looking it over.

"I'm here to do a follow-up on the trial." Bren stares at him, blankly. "The Buddy Allen-Carter Singleton story."

"Well, I'm probably not the best one to talk to."

"My brother Harold's a music producer, lots of new bands are coming to his studio. And he's looking for songs."

He finally has Bren's attention. "Really?"

"Bren Lace, right? I think you've got lots of talent, sweetheart." He hands her another card. "Look, if you're ever in Dallas, call me. I'll introduce you. Like I say, he may be looking for someone like you."

Bren gives Kirchner her best smile. "Well, sir, thank you. I just happen to be heading to Dallas soon. So, I'll definitely be in touch!"

Bren watches intently as Kirchner disappears into the crowd. Blaze and Parker immediately rush up to her. "My, my," Parker teases in his cattiest voice, "*Who was that dirty old man?*"

"Could be my fairy godfather," she replies, stuffing a chocolate chip cookie in her mouth.

Less than a week later, Jonny stands in his front yard, watching as Vic Chandler loads Jonny's suitcase in the trunk of the Sparks family Chevy. "I think we're all set," Vic calls out. He steps back to contemplate the car. "It's a far cry from my Roadster but hopefully, it's roadworthy."

Janet, standing near the back door, chimes in: "It only has to get us to the airport."

"*And back,*" Vic adds. "What's Oklahoma City, about 160 miles, roundtrip?"

Jonny turns his attention to Bren, waiting patiently a few yards away. "I guess it's time," he says, trying not to look her in the eye.

Bren walks up to Jonny and hands him a slip of paper. "Here's my address in Dallas. I should be there in a couple weeks. I'd love to hear from you."

"Of course!" Jonny replies, shoving it into his back pocket. He pulls a folded sheet of paper from his jacket. "Here. I, uh, wrote you another poem. Don't know if you'll like it, but it's the way I feel."

He nervously hands it to her. Bren starts to look it over, then gives it back to him. "Please read it to me."

Jonny's been in this situation with her before, but it doesn't make it any easier. He takes a deep breath, then delivers the words as best he can:

"I treasure every moment we're together
I measure every moment as forever
My love for you is boundless – flowing like a stream
I'll catch you in the ocean of my dreams."

Bren throws her arms around him and hugs him tightly. "I love it," she whispers, "Thank you. *For everything.*" Jonny tires to speak, but can't. Bren grips his hands. "Jonny, I love you so much, so much I had to let you go. I hope you understand that."

He nods and gives her a last, longing look – then turns and walks briskly toward the car, determined not to glance back. Janet and Vic stand together, arm-in-arm, watching him approach. But he can barely see them through his tears.

Revised Forecast

"The best way to make your dreams come true is to wake up."

Cassius Clay
(a.k.a. Muhammad Ali)

Herman Lace here. Back again. And you thought you were rid of me!

To be honest, I was mighty angry when Mayor Thomas closed Medicine Park High. I think it had more to do with his personal agenda than the fact the building was collapsing. But there you go. I took a deep breath and moved on…started teaching at Eisenhower in Lawton. I spent more than a decade there before retiring. I liked it, all in all. Same knuckleheads, different hallways.

You know, when you finally hang it up, there's time to take stock. I imagine my small-town life looks narrow to you. I mean, Medicine Park never had more than a thousand people, even in its hey-day. It's been a pretty simple life. But in my defense, I tried to keep my eyes open. Stay awake. See the big picture.

Take that whole Vietnam fiasco. I saw it coming, early on. Folks around here didn't see the lies for years. Even after Wilton Tate's oldest son, Tyson, came home in a box, a Green Beret with a chest full of medals. Unfortunately, he also had a back full of shrapnel. Goodness gracious. They called Vietnam 'McNamara's war.' When President Kennedy named Bob McNamara Secretary of Defense, it was the best thing that ever happened to Ford Motors. They finally got rid of him. McNamara presided over the launch of the Edsel, which you may recall, was a total bomb. And after he left, they rolled out the Mustang, a major success. There's an analogy in there somewhere with a dash of irony, I suppose.

Another thing I saw coming: the assassination of Martin Luther King. But to be fair, anyone could see that. I mean, you've got a festering cesspool of angry, ignorant rednecks, their lives are going nowhere. Then they see 'uppity colored folks' moving to the front of the line. It doesn't play well. People like

James Earl Ray are *pathetic*. But I hate to say: racists like him'll be with us for a long, long time.

I'll tell ya what I *didn't* see coming: Back in '62, when Kennedy pledged to get us to the moon, I thought he was *howling at it*. Turns out, it only took seven years before Armstrong planted our flag up there. Of course, Nixon tried to take credit for the whole thing. I gotta say: I saw Tricky Dick coming miles away, long before he reached the White House. And I had the good fortune to see him chased out of it.

Anyway, now that I've got time on my hands, I finally started that book about Medicine Park. The one I talked about for so long. At first, it was gonna be about the underhanded things the mayor and his cohorts were doing. All the deception beneath the surface. But I decided to go in another direction…focus on the crazy things that happened back in late '63, early '64. Like Sampson Whitefeather's disappearance. And *reappearance*. And the Buddy Allen trial. And don't forget those thousands of dead fish!

Like Dickens wrote: '*It was the best of times and the worst of times.*' For me, the worst part was when my daughter, Bren, finally left the nest. I know she had to go out and seek her fortune. Hell, I wish *I'd* done that. Anyway, I always figured she'd be successful. But it hurts. It still feels mighty empty, her living so far away.

A final confession: There for a while, I considered going back to the bottle. You know, drowning myself to stay afloat. So far, I've resisted the temptation. The truth is, no matter how you slice it, that kind of approach is bad medicine.

Herman Lace

Medicine Park, OK

September 6, 1978

To Bren Lace, Benton Illinois looks and feels the same in 1984 as it did the day she first arrived back in 1963. *Something else* that hasn't changed: every summer, she spends a few frustrating days with her mom, who still resides in Benton with her sister Doris.

Arriving from New York on this unseasonably cool afternoon in July, Bren scrutinizes her mother, Carol, as she emotionally smothers Bren's nine-year-old daughter. "Deborah, you're much too thin!" Carol exclaims, the moment her granddaughter emerges from their rental car. "We need to fatten you up!"

Her granddaughter responds with an overly theatrical eye roll. Bren watches in dismay as her aunt Doris helps her mother negotiate her walker. Although Carol's no longer prone to radical mood swings, she's in rapidly-declining health – and at age 66, is obsessed with her inevitable demise.

It's now 4:30 and time for *Jeopardy!* The highlight of Doris and Carol's day. And, of course, Carol insists that her granddaughter watch every minute with her – sitting as close to her as possible. During the entire 30-minute program, Bren wonders whether she and Deborah should re-pack their suitcases and trade a local motel room for the cramped, stuffy guestroom in the back of the house.

And then, it happened: At the end of *Jeopardy*, Doris, remote control in hand, flips to channel four and the CBS logo appears on the screen, followed by a voice-over announcer.

"And now, live from KMOX-TV, here's your 'Eye on St. Louis' News-4 anchor, Jonathon Sparks!" Bren, walking toward the kitchen, stops on a dime, wheeling around to check out the charismatic newsman behind the desk. As the camera pushes in for a close-up, Bren whispers to herself, "It's him – his face, his voice – everything!" While Jonathon Sparks delivers the day's top stories, Bren concocts a good one of her own: She'll get in touch with him at the station and schedule a dinner date. And even though Benton to St. Louis is just a 90-minute drive, after twenty years, she hopes the distance between them isn't too great.

Two nights later, Bren sits at a table inside Dominic's Italian restaurant, located in a venerable St. Louis neighborhood called *The Hill*. As she waits for her special date to arrive, she sips a glass of Chardonnay and surveys the elegant decor – with its dark maple paneling, detailed crown molding, and elaborately-framed Impressionist prints. Bren also notices that the patrons are conservatively dressed, and she wonders if her silver linen pant suit, with its padded shoulders, is too trendy for a Midwestern city.

Then he arrives. The maître d' escorts Jonny Sparks, wearing a navy-blue Brooks Brothers suit, to her table. As Bren stands to greet him, Jon clutches her in a bear hug and swings her around, several inches off the ground. "Whoa!" Bren chuckles. "You must be glad to see me!"

"Thrilled," Jonny replies. "And you look as beautiful as ever."

"Not bad for the mother of a nine-year-old," Bren replies as the maître d' pulls the chair out for her.

"Yeah, when you called, I was surprised you'd returned to Benton. Especially with your daughter along."

"It's all about my mother," Bren replies, sarcastically. "Some things never change." Jonny takes the wine list from the sommelier. Bren reaches across the table and squeezes his hand. "By the way, sorry to hear about your mom."

He forces a smile. "Thanks. She was doing so well too till the cancer moved in. She went really fast."

"Pancreatic, you said?"

Jonny nods. "At least she and Vic got to take that Alaskan cruise they kept talking about. They seemed really happy together."

"And Vic? What's he doing now?"

Jonny laughs. "The last I heard, he's a partner with Wilton Tate. In the quarter horse business."

"You're kidding!" This completely takes Bren by surprise. "What about…what happened to Ben Thomas?"

"Oh, he's mixed up in it somehow. After four years of my mom breathing down his neck, you know, as County Commissioner, I think he decided politics wasn't fun anymore. Couldn't make enough money with Mom around."

They both laugh heartily, enjoying the thought of it all. The waiter arrives, and Jonny convinces Bren to let him order some house specialties for them to share. After the sommelier returns for their wine order, Jonny asks Bren about her father, Herman. "Oh, he passed away about 18 months ago. No surprise there. He was too contentious for this world."

Jonny nods. "Definitely a character." Suddenly, a thought: "Hey, you know who I was thinking about the other day? *Blaze Whitefeather.*"

"Ah, yes, Blaze! You know, the last I heard, he and his dad – Sampson – applied for an Indian casino license in Lawton. I think there's a legal fight about it, but it looks like the courts are gonna let the tribes get into gaming. Wouldn't you know? If there's an angle to exploit, you can count on Blaze!"

Somewhere in the middle of their entrees, Jonny decides to query Bren about her recent divorce. "Oh, not *that* recent," she replies. "It's been going on for a couple of years, back and forth. It became final about, oh, a little over nine months ago."

"Wasn't he your songwriting partner?"

"Still is! The weird thing about it; we're working together even better now. We just finished a score for a Broadway musical, going into rehearsals next month."

"Wow. That's exciting."

Bren smiles, nods. "You, uh, never told me about *you*, Jon. Are you married?"

"Never got married. I came dangerously close a few times, but."

"Let me guess: Never met the right girl?"

"*Oh, I've met her.* I just couldn't catch her."

After dinner, Jonny drives Bren to St. Louis' Gateway Park for a late-evening stroll. It's a clear, calm summer night as they walk beneath the soaring stainless-steel arch, built to symbolize American expansionism, the kind of 'manifest destiny' Bren's father railed against in his history classes.

Bren invites Jonny to sit beside her on the grass the arch directly overhead, and the rushing Mississippi River in view a short distance to the east. Jonny takes her by the hand. "You know, Bren, something I always wondered."

"Yes?"

"How were you able to write such good songs back then at such an early age?"

Bren chuckles. "You're the first one who's ever asked me that! Hmm. I guess people assume it's something I was born with."

"That's what I always thought. God-given talent."

Bren thinks a moment. "Well, I never told anyone this. When I was little, maybe six or seven, my grandmother gave me a jar, you know, one of those pint mason jars, filled with water from Medicine Creek. She believed the water had mystical powers, probably because of those old tribal legends."

"Yeah, I think I heard something about that."

"So, most nights, after lights out, I took a sip from the jar, stashed under my bed. And then, I'd let the magic potion transport me to a special place, where I'd imagine all kinds of things. You know, stories. Create conversations in my head. And, sometimes, phrases or ideas would come to me, outta the blue, and the next day I'd write 'em down. And when I started playing piano during my stay in Benton, I'd hear melodies, too."

"Are you saying you took creek water with you to Benton?"

Bren laughs. "No, in fact, I stopped drinking the stuff long before that. I realized I didn't need the water, it just, in the beginning, it helped me open my mind up to other things, new possibilities. To believe in the magic."

"The magic?"

"Yeah. What I eventually called '*The Creative Intelligence of the Universe.*' And once I trusted that power that I could access it on my own, that all I needed was silent meditation *and belief* well, it never left. And I rely on it, even to this day. And I never worry about it going away because the songs and ideas don't come from me. They vibrate through the universe, in fragments, on higher frequencies. All I do is tune in and catch them."

Jonny sits, quietly, taking it all in. And it's a lot.

Bren finally breaks the silence. "What about you, Jonny? What about those great poems you wrote me back then? Where'd *they* come from?"

He shrugs. "I dunno. I think you inspired me. I was simply expressing how I felt, being around you." He considers this. "You know, they started coming to me after I had those dreams after almost drowning that night on Founder's Lake."

Bren's eyes light up. "Yeah, you mentioned having strange visions! Trips, almost."

"I had several weird experiences like that but to tell you the truth, I never trusted them. They scared me too much and I eventually shut 'em down."

Bren considers this. "Well, it's not too late, Jonny to, you know, open up to them again. To access a consciousness beyond your own."

"I'm not sure how to do that. I mean, how do *you* do it?"

"Silence. Stillness. Trust. Believing in a world beyond our perceptions, in a force infinitely greater than ourselves."

Jonny's mind begins to drift away – recalling what his dream-world shaman, his native spiritual guide – told him twenty years ago back in Medicine Park: "The creek flows into the lake and the river spills into the sea and the sea cascades into the ocean. And when we die, our individual consciousness flows back out into the universe, where it all started from the beginning."

Jonny grabs Bren's hand and helps her to her feet. They start walking southward, parallel to the river, the faint sound of the Mississippi flowing past them in the dark. Just like the river, Jonny's mind streams back to what Vic Chandler told his mother so long ago, *Time bends and loops and circles around and round, like the seasons.*"

Jonny smiles, a feeling of joy sweeping over him. He realizes: "Here we are after all these years, circling around, together again. Bren's someone I always believed in. And as miraculous as it seems, she believed in me! Now she's inviting me to believe in something much bigger than ourselves, something greater than we can imagine – *beyond time* – always there to guide us, even before we met back in Medicine Park."

Was Medicine Park even real? Or did we just create it in our minds?

– THE END –

(Which, of course, loops to the beginning.)

Milton Keynes UK
Ingram Content Group UK Ltd.
UKHW022042301123
433577UK00010B/633